SNAP REVISION

THE SIGN OF THE FOUR

AQA GCSE 9-1 English Literature

RACHEL GRANT

REVISE SET TEXTS IN A SNAP

Published by Collins
An imprint of HarperCollinsPublishers
1 London Bridge Street,
London, SE1 9GF

9780008306632

First published 2018

10 9 8 7 6 5 4 3 2 1

British Library Cataloguing in Publication Data.

A CIP record of this book is available from the
British Library.

Printed and bound in China by RR Donnelley APS

Commissioning Editor: Gillian Bowman
Managing Editor: Craig Balfour
Author: Rachel Grant
Proofreader: Jill Laidlaw
Project manager and editor:
   Project One Publishing Solutions, Scotland
Typesetting: Jouve
Cover designers: Kneath Associates and
   Sarah Duxbury
Production: Lyndsey Rogers

ACKNOWLEDGEMENTS

The author and publisher are grateful to the
copyright holders for permission to use quoted
materials and images.

Every effort has been made to trace copyright
holders and obtain their permission for the use of
copyright material. The author and publisher will
gladly receive information enabling them to rectify
any error or omission in subsequent editions. All
facts are correct at time of going to press.

Contents

Chapters 1 and 2

You must be able to: understand what happens in Chapters 1 and 2.

What do we learn from the opening chapter?

Holmes and Watson have lived together in Baker Street for several years. Having no case at present, Holmes relieves his boredom by taking cocaine. Being a doctor, Watson disapproves of the habit.

Holmes shows how, though observation, he can **deduce** that Watson has sent a telegraph that morning. Watson tests Holmes's theories of deduction by asking him to examine and deduce facts about Watson's watch. Holmes does so, but Watson is upset when Holmes gives an accurate account of Watson's dissolute brother, now dead.

Mary Morstan is announced.

What is Holmes's new case?

Mary Morstan explains the case. She has received a letter from an 'unknown friend' asking her to meet that night. She narrates the history leading up to this. Ten years before, her father Captain Morstan arrived in England on leave from service in India. Mary was 17 and at boarding school in Edinburgh; her mother was dead.

Before Mary could meet her father in London, he mysteriously disappeared without trace, leaving his luggage at the hotel.

To Mary's knowledge he had only one friend in town, Major Sholto, who was in the same regiment.

Major Sholto claimed not to know that his friend Captain Morstan was back in England.

Six years ago, Mary received a large pearl by post. Every year since on 4 May, another pearl has arrived, but never with a note. Now she has received the mysterious letter, referring to her as 'a wronged woman' and promising that she 'shall have justice'.

The letter is postmarked SW London, 7 July. Holmes examines the handwriting carefully.

Holmes and Watson agree to accompany Mary to the rendezvous at the Lyceum Theatre at 7pm. The letter specifies that no police should be involved.

Holmes leaves to consult some references. Watson entertains romantic thoughts about Mary but reminds himself he is no catch – he has little money and a weak leg.

Key Quotations to Learn

His great powers ... made me diffident and backward in crossing him. (Watson, about Holmes: Chapter 1)

'I never guess. It is a shocking habit – destructive to the logical faculty.' (Holmes: Chapter 1)

I confess, too, that I was irritated by the egotism ... (Chapter 1)

Summary

- Holmes is bored because he has no case to solve.
- He entertains himself by taking cocaine and demonstrating his powers of deduction to Watson.
- Mary Morstan explains that on every 4th May for the past six years she has been sent a pearl by post.
- Today she has received a letter from an 'unknown friend', asking her to be outside the Lyceum Theatre at 7pm.
- She must not bring police but may bring two friends.
- Holmes and Watson agree to accompany her.

Questions

QUICK TEST
1. How does Watson test Holmes's powers of deduction?
2. When did Captain Morstan disappear?
3. What does Mary Morstan receive by post every year?
4. Who is Major Sholto?
5. Who claims Mary Morstan is 'a wronged woman'?

EXAM PRACTICE
Using one or more of the 'Key Quotations to Learn', write a paragraph explaining how Conan Doyle establishes the relationship between Holmes and Watson.

You must be able to: understand what happens in Chapters 3 and 4.

What is 'the sign of the four'?

From obituaries in *The Times*, Holmes has discovered that Major Sholto died on 28 April 1882. He deduces that Mary must have been deprived of something belonging to her father: she received the first pearl one week after Sholto died. Sholto's heir wishes to compensate her loss.

However, he cannot explain why Sholto's heir wishes to meet Mary now.

On the way to the Lyceum Theatre, Mary produces a plan found in her father's desk. It shows a large building marked with a small cross in red ink, '3.37 from left' in pencil, and the words 'The sign of the four – Jonathan Small, Mahomet Singh, Abdullah Khan, Dost Akbar'.

Holmes pronounces the paper to be Indian.

At the Lyceum, the three are transferred to a different cab and set off to an unknown destination.

Watson loses track of their direction, but Holmes does not. They draw up at a drab house in south London. A Hindoo (Hindu) servant shows them in.

What is Thaddeus Sholto's story?

Mr Thaddeus Sholto is a small, bald, nervous man who lives in great luxury. He tells them that his father, Major Sholto, retired from the Indian Army a wealthy man. He lived with his twin sons, Thaddeus and Bartholomew, at Pondicherry Lodge. The sons were aware that their father lived in fear. He employed prize-fighters as porters, and once fired a pistol at a wooden-legged man.

On receiving a letter from India in April 1882, Major Sholto fell terminally ill. On his deathbed, he told his sons how Captain Morstan died.

Before he could tell his sons where the treasure was hidden, Sholto saw a man's face at the window that terrified him so much, he died. The man was not found but next morning there was a note on Sholto's corpse: 'The sign of the four'.

How did Captain Morstan die?

Morstan met Sholto at Pondicherry Lodge. They argued about how to divide their treasure, acquired in India. Morstan had a seizure and fell. Hitting his head against the corner of the treasure chest, he died.

In panic, Sholto covered it up. He and his servant Lal Rao buried Morstan's body.

How was the treasure discovered?

The brothers searched the house and dug up the grounds for the treasure, but in vain. Only one piece remained – a pearl **chaplet**. They agreed to send one pearl each year to Mary to recompense her for her loss. The brothers subsequently argued about this however, and parted.

Now Thaddeus has learned that Bartholomew has found the treasure in a secret garret. It is worth at least half a million pounds.

The four set off for Pondicherry Lodge.

Key Quotations to Learn

[The] monster tentacles which the giant city was throwing out into the country. (Chapter 3)

In that sorry house it looked as out of place as a diamond of the first water in a setting of brass. (Thaddeus' apartment: Chapter 4)

'It was a bearded, hairy face, with wild cruel eyes and an expression of concentrated malevolence.' (Thaddeus Sholto: Chapter 4)

Summary

- Holmes connects the pearls to Sholto's death.
- Mary shows them a plan signed by 'The sign of the four'.
- Thaddeus tells the story of the hidden treasure and how Morstan died.
- A mysterious letter from India and a terrifying face at the window scare Sholto to death.
- Bartholomew has found the treasure in a hidden garret.

Questions

QUICK TEST
1. What are the names of 'the four'?
2. Who did Sholto employ as porters?
3. What did Sholto see at the window just before he died?
4. Who sent the pearls to Mary?
5. Where was the treasure hidden?

EXAM PRACTICE
Using one or more of the 'Key Quotations to Learn', write a paragraph explaining how Conan Doyle builds suspense in these chapters.

Chapters 5 and 6

You must be able to: understand what happens in Chapters 5 and 6.

What is at Pondicherry Lodge?

Outside Pondicherry Lodge their way is barred by the porter, McMurdo. He allows Thaddeus to enter, but no one else. Bartholomew has been in his room all day.

Holmes reminds McMurdo they have met before when Holmes beat him in a fist fight. McMurdo allows them to enter the grounds. They hear the sound of a whimpering woman – the housekeeper. Thaddeus goes to Bartholomew's room.

Watson and Mary hold hands – a touching and romantic moment for Watson.

As they survey the mounds of dirt left from the treasure search, Thaddeus bursts out of the house in terror: there is something wrong with Bartholomew. Holmes and Watson slowly ascend with him to Bartholomew's room, which his locked on the inside.

Through the keyhole, Holmes and Watson see the dead face of Bartholomew as if suspended in darkness. They force the door open. Inside is chemical equipment, steps to a hole in the ceiling, and a rope.

On the table next to the dead man's hand is a roughly made hammer-like object and a note: 'The sign of the four'.

Holmes finds a long black thorn (dart) beneath the dead man's ear: he has been poisoned.

Thaddeus panics: the treasure has gone and, as he was the last person to see his brother alive, he will be the prime suspect in the murder. Holmes sends him to report the crime to the police.

What does Holmes deduce?

Holmes gets to work, observing circular, muddy marks on the floor and table, deducing they were made by a wooden stump which, together with other boot marks, indicate they are the prints of a man with a wooden leg.

This man could not scale the outside wall and therefore, Holmes deduces, an accomplice must have let a rope down from above to enable him to enter the window.

Further examination leads Holmes to conclude the accomplice came through the hole in the ceiling. Ascending, Holmes and Watson find a trapdoor to the roof – and prints of a naked foot: human, but child-sized. One of these is edged in creosote (a smelly chemical used to preserve wood).

Holmes points out that the thorn that killed Bartholomew was fired from the hole in the ceiling; the thorn is foreign, it has been trimmed, and it was fired with little force.

Sholto returns with police inspector Athelney Jones and Holmes tells him the facts. Athelney jumps to the wrong conclusion and arrests Thaddeus. From the clues he has found so far, Holmes deduces that one of the intruders is Jonathan Small (one of the four names on Mary's map).

Holmes sends Watson to escort Mary home, and tells him to return with a dog named Toby. Holmes intends to use Toby as a sniffer dog to find the intruders.

Key Quotations to Learn

Holmes whipped his lens out of his pocket and carefully examined marks which appeared to me to be mere shapeless smudges ... (Chapter 5)

He walked slowly from step to step ... shooting keen glances to right and left. (Chapter 5)

'I only require a few missing links to have an entirely connected case.' (Holmes: Chapter 5)

'How often have I said to you that when you have eliminated the impossible, whatever remains, *however improbable*, must be the truth?' (Holmes: Chapter 6)

Summary

- Bartholomew is found dead in a room locked on the inside.
- He was murdered with a poisoned thorn.
- The treasure is missing.
- Holmes uses footprints to profile the two intruders.
- Athelney Jones arrests Thaddeus.
- The wooden-legged intruder is Jonathan Small.
- Holmes sends Watson for a sniffer dog.

Questions

QUICK TEST
1. What is strange about Bartholomew's room?
2. How do they first see his body?
3. What is strange about the naked footprints?
4. How did the wooden-legged man get into the room?
5. What does Holmes want Watson to bring back?

EXAM PRACTICE
Using one or more of the 'Key Quotations to Learn', write a paragraph analysing how Conan Doyle demonstrates Holmes's detective skills in these two chapters.

Chapters 7 and 8

You must be able to: understand what happens in Chapters 7 and 8.

Where does Toby lead Holmes and Watson at first?

Watson takes Mary home and collects the dog Toby from Pinchin Lane, as Holmes had asked.

Watson contemplates the extraordinary events of the night (it is now the early hours of the morning). When he returns with Toby he finds Holmes still working. Holmes has examined the naked footprints; they have splayed toes, unlike Holmes's own.

Sholto and McMurdo have been arrested and detained in police custody.

Holmes retraces the mystery accomplice's steps across the roof and finds a pouch with thorns inside it. They are like the dart that killed Bartholomew.

Using a handkerchief soaked in creosote, Holmes gives Toby the scent. As dawn breaks the dog leads them northwards, across and through south London. As they walk, Holmes summarises the facts of the case so far: not only has he identified Small, he has also worked out why and how Morstan and Sholto became involved and what motivated Small to visit Bartholomew after he found the treasure. Holmes does not think Small wanted to kill Bartholomew. Holmes thinks Small was annoyed when the accomplice did this.

Toby follows the scent to a barrel on a hand-trolley, which is smeared with creosote. Holmes and Watson collapse with laughter at the dog's mistake.

How does Holmes use the 'Baker Street irregulars'?

Toby regains the scent and leads them to a wharf. Holmes questions Mrs Smith, who lives in the house there. Her husband Mordecai has been away since the previous morning. He and their eldest son Jim took off in their steam launch, the *Aurora*. With apparently casual questioning, Holmes learns from her that a 'wooden-legged man' with an 'ugly face' has been calling for her husband and is now a passenger on the launch. Mrs Smith does not trust this man.

Holmes gets a detailed description of the launch and they return to Baker Street. On the way Holmes sends a telegraph summoning his 'dirty little lieutenant, Wiggins'. Over breakfast Holmes entertains Watson with a newspaper report of the crime.

Wiggins arrives with his group of street urchins – the Baker Street irregulars – and Holmes instructs them to send word as soon as one of them sights the *Aurora*.

Holmes reveals what he has concluded about Small's mysterious accomplice: he is probably a native of the Andaman Islands as the description of those people in the latest gazetteer (an atlas or directory, which Holmes has at hand) exactly matches the clues found in the locked room (small feet, stone-headed clubs, poisoned arrows).

Realising that Watson now needs sleep, Holmes plays some soft music on his violin. As he falls asleep, Watson thinks of Mary.

Key Quotations to Learn

'The answer is obvious.' (Holmes to Watson: Chapter 7)

'It is the only hypothesis which covers the facts. Let us see how it fits in with the sequel.' (Holmes to Watson: Chapter 7)

'Does the reasoning strike you as being faulty?' (Holmes to Watson: Chapter 7)

Summary

- After following the wrong scent, Toby leads them to a wharf on the river.
- They learn that Mordecai Smith has taken a wooden-legged man as passenger on his steam ship the *Aurora*.
- Holmes dispatches the Baker Street irregulars to track down the *Aurora*.
- Holmes concludes that Small's accomplice is a native of the Andaman Islands.

Questions

QUICK TEST
1. What does Holmes notice about the naked footprints, compared to his own?
2. What is used to give Toby the scent?
3. What is the name of Smith's steam launch?
4. Who is the leader of the Baker Street irregulars?
5. Where does the small-footed man come from?

EXAM PRACTICE
Using one or more of the 'Key Quotations to Learn', write a paragraph explaining how Conan Doyle presents Holmes's hypothesis.

You must be able to: understand what happens in Chapters 9 to 11.

Who picks up the trail of the *Aurora*?

They wait for news but the Irregulars cannot find the launch. Watson visits Mary, who is more worried about Thaddeus than the treasure, although she stands to gain by its recovery.

Holmes grows restless. He has widened the search, but another day passes. On the third morning he goes off himself, dressed as a sailor.

Next morning Watson reads that Thaddeus has been released. He notices that Holmes has placed an advert in the paper, asking for information about Mordecai Smith and the *Aurora*.

Holmes sends Jones a telegram telling him to go to Baker Street. Holmes has tracked down the *Aurora*. An old sailor arrives, looking for Holmes. They wait for Holmes, then the sailor reveals his identity – it is Holmes, in disguise!

Holmes asks Jones to have a police launch with two policemen at Westminster Stairs at 7pm. Jones will catch the criminals, Watson will take the unopened treasure box to Mary, and Holmes will interview Jonathan Small. Jones agrees.

How do they catch the *Aurora*?

Armed with pistols, they set off for Jacobson's Yard on the police launch. Holmes recounts how he used probability to pick up the trail: putting himself in Small's shoes, Holmes reasoned that Small would need to hide before fleeing the country. The launch too needed to be hidden, and what better place than in a repair yard? Following this line of thinking, Holmes found the launch at Jacobson's Yard. He overheard Mordecai Smith who revealed they could expect the gang at 8pm.

One of Holmes's boys will give a signal when the launch takes off. Holmes plans to capture it on the river.

When the *Aurora* appears, they give chase. Even at full speed they take time to draw level. At last they get a clear view of the wooden-legged man and the little dark man. They take aim, and Holmes tells Watson to fire if the little man raises his hand. The little man draws out a blowpipe and puts it to his lips. They both fire, and the little man falls into the river.

The wooden-legged man runs the launch into the bank but his wooden leg sinks into the mud; he cannot escape. They drag him onto the police launch, collect the Smiths, and stow the treasure box.

Holmes finds a poisoned dart stuck in the wood behind where they had been standing.

What is in the box?

Small explains that Tonga murdered Bartholomew against Small's wishes and clears the Smiths.

The treasure box is locked. Small has thrown the key in the river. Watson takes the box to Mary, who appears unmoved by the idea of being rich. When Watson breaks it open, it's empty – but Mary remains calm. Watson declares his love for her and she accepts him.

Key Quotations to Learn

The furnaces roared, and the powerful engines whizzed and clanked, like a great metallic heart. ... With every throb of the engines we sprang and quivered like a living thing. (Chapter 10)

'Pile it on, men, pile it on!' cried Holmes ... (Chapter 10)

[Never] did sport give me such a wild thrill as this mad, flying man-hunt down the Thames. (Chapter 10)

Summary

- Holmes goes in search of the *Aurora*.
- Having tracked it down, Holmes uses police resources to lie in wait on the river.
- They chase the *Aurora* downriver.
- They shoot the little man dead, capture Small and the Smiths, and recover the treasure box.
- The treasure box is empty.

Questions

QUICK TEST
1. Why does Holmes himself decide to track down the *Aurora*?
2. Where does he finally find the *Aurora*?
3. What disguise does Holmes adopt?
4. What two things does Jones promise in return for capturing the criminals?
5. How do they capture Small?

EXAM PRACTICE
Using one or more of the 'Key Quotations to Learn', write a paragraph analysing how Conan Doyle conveys a sense of excitement during the river chase.

Chapter 12

You must be able to: understand what happens in Chapter 12.

Why did Small go to Agra?

Small explains he threw the treasure overboard. He calls this 'justice' for the sign of four – for they and no one else deserved the treasure.

He tells his story: he joined the army at 18 and went to India. He was bitten by a crocodile while swimming and lost his leg. He could still ride a horse, so worked on a plantation near Muttra, close to the border of the Northwest Provinces. At the time of the Indian Rebellion, Muttra was right in the path of the Indian rebels. However, the plantation owner refused to leave.

One day Small returned to find the plantation owner and wife murdered. Small was attacked and rode to Agra to find safety, but it was surrounded by rebels.

How did 'the four' come together?

Small joined the guard at Agra Fort with two Sikh troopers under his **command**. One night, the Sikhs turned on Small. One of them, Abdullah Khan, threatened to kill him if he did not help them steal the Agra treasure – if he did help, he would have a fair share.

Khan told Small the treasure belonged to a rajah (an Indian king or prince) and was being carried to Agra by a trusted servant. With him was Dost Akbar, Khan's relative – who must also take a share of the treasure. Akbar would lead the treasure to them.

The servant arrived and Small turned him over to the Sikhs. In the scuffle, Small aided the Sikhs by tripping the servant, and they murdered him.

Having counted the treasure, they stowed the box in a wall. Small drew four plans of the spot, each signed 'the sign of the four'.

Once peace was restored, 'the four' were found guilty of murder and imprisoned.

Why did Small swear vengeance on Sholto?

Small was transferred to the Andaman Islands. He met Morstan and Sholto. Sholto lost heavily at cards and Small approached him with a plan to recover the treasure. With Morstan, Sholto agreed to fetch the treasure and send a boat for 'the four'.

Sholto double-crossed them and returned to England with the treasure, leaving the prisoners to rot.

Small earned the loyalty of a native Andaman (named Tonga) by saving his life after he was attacked by a convict gang. Tonga helped him escape and Small tracked Sholto down. When Sholto died, Small left the note but couldn't find the treasure. The rest of the story is as Holmes concluded: Tonga murdered Bartholomew, and Small made off with the treasure.

Watson tells Holmes he is to marry Mary. Holmes is exhausted but explains that Lal Rao was Small's confederate at the house. The story finishes as it started, with Holmes reaching for cocaine.

Key Quotations to Learn

'If you want to hear my story, I have no wish to hold it back.' (Small: Chapter 12)

'Black or blue,' said I, 'they are in with me, and we all go together.' (Small: Chapter 12)

'I took him in hand, though he was venomous as a young snake.' (Small, about Tonga: Chapter 12)

Summary

- As a young soldier in India, Small lost his leg to a crocodile attack while swimming.
- He worked on a plantation but fled to Agra during the Indian Rebellion.
- He joined with three Sikhs to steal the Agra treasure.
- 'The four' were later imprisoned for murder.
- Sholto and Morstan agreed to retrieve the treasure and rescue 'the four' but Sholto double-crossed them all.
- Back in England, Small and Tonga tracked Sholto down.
- Tonga killed Bartholomew and Small took the treasure.

Questions

QUICK TEST
1. What event prompted Small to go to Agra?
2. Who told Small about the treasure?
3. What did they do with the treasure?
4. Why did Small approach Sholto?
5. How did Small earn Tonga's loyalty?

EXAM PRACTICE
Using one or more of the 'Key Quotations to Learn', write a paragraph analysing why Conan Doyle chose to include Small's story.

Narrator and Narrative Structure

You must be able to: explain the significance of the narrator and the narrative structure Conan Doyle uses in the novel.

Why does Conan Doyle choose Dr Watson as narrator?

As readers we must be able to trust Watson. We rely on him to give a truthful, honest (but not unbiased) account. Watson is male, white, middle class and a doctor – all attributes which to Victorian readers made him trustworthy and a reliable source of information and judgement.

Watson is a **first-person narrator**. This means he gives his own **subjective point of view**. He is not **omniscient**. For example, when Holmes goes off disguised as a sailor, like Watson we wait for news. We know nothing of Holmes's movements during this time. This device enables Conan Doyle to build suspense.

Using Watson as the narrator helps Conan Doyle to reveal and conceal information from the reader. Watson is Holmes's trusted assistant, privy to some, but not all, of Holmes's actions and deductions. Watson sees the clues but does not have Holmes's detective skills. This puts readers in the same situation as Watson: the clues are revealed, but not joined up.

Despite having great respect for his friend, Watson is not blind to his faults. In Chapter 9, Watson starts to doubt Holmes. This moment of doubt adds to Watson's credibility as narrator – it shows that he is being completely honest.

How does Conan Doyle present the timeline?

The events of the novel are carefully plotted, and the timeline is skilfully handled by Conan Doyle. The present-day story takes place over just four days in September 1888. The first eight chapters take place over a single day and night, and include two **flashbacks**:

- Mary's story (Chapter 2) goes back to 1878
- Thaddeus' story (Chapter 4) goes back 11 years.

The past events in these **recounts** contain important information and clues that help Holmes to start to unravel the case (Chapter 5). Conan Doyle uses flashback again:

- Small's story (Chapter 11) goes back four days
- Small's story (Chapter 12) goes back to his birth.

Why does Conan Doyle use flashbacks?

A detective must be prepared to piece together past events, and to solve this case facts and events that occurred more than 30 years previously (such as the four stealing the treasure) are connected to recent events (like the pearls sent to Mary). Conan Doyle uses flashbacks to reveal, piece by piece, important details from the past. It's a structural technique that builds suspense, and it invites readers to piece together evidence and solve the crime as if they too are detectives.

Key Quotations to Learn

'Briefly,' she continued, 'the facts are these.' (Mary: Chapter 2)

'I can only lay the facts before you as far as I know them myself.' (Thaddeus: Chapter 4)

Could there be, I wondered, some radical flaw in my companion's reasoning? (Chapter 9)

'What I say to you is God's truth, every word of it.' (Small: Chapter 12)

Summary

- Watson is a first-person narrator. He does not know or understand everything that Holmes does.
- Using Watson as narrator enables Conan Doyle to reveal and conceal information from readers.
- Conan Doyle uses flashbacks to reveal information from the past needed to explain the present case.
- Flashbacks keep readers engaged, because they want to understand the whole story.

Questions

QUICK TEST
1. Who is the narrator of the novel?
2. What type of narrator is this?
3. What is the timeframe of the present-day events?
4. Which characters tell their stories in flashbacks?
5. Why does the author use flashbacks?

EXAM PRACTICE
Using one or more of the 'Key Quotations to Learn', write a paragraph explaining how Conan Doyle uses flashback to structure the novel.

London in 1888

You must be able to: understand how Conan Doyle presents aspects of late-Victorian London in the novel.

What was it like to live in London?

At this time, London was an overcrowded city where poverty and squalor existed side by side with wealth and luxury. From 1861 to 1910, London's population grew from 3 million to more than 7 million and this huge influx of people resulted in overcrowded housing and poor sanitation, placing great strain on public amenities like roads and sewerage systems. Rising crime was a problem. The suburbs expanded rapidly.

In Chapter 2 Watson gives a vivid description of a foggy, drizzly, muddy, dreary, crowded scene as they ride in a cab down the Strand. He depicts London as overcrowded, dirty and miserable, a sight that he finds depressing.

When they reach the new suburbs of south London, Watson describes the 'monster tentacles' of 'dull brick' terraces. In contrast, Thaddeus Sholto's house is opulently furnished, 'an oasis of art in the howling desert of south London'. The contrast between ugliness/poverty and beauty/wealth is stark.

Why do we meet characters from other countries?

The population of London has always been a melting pot of people from different countries and cultures; at this time, lots of them were immigrants from the British Empire colonies, drawn to the city in search of opportunity. Conan Doyle presents several such characters who seem 'incongruous' in the London setting: a Hindoo (Hindu) servant opens the door to Thaddeus Sholto's house; Major Sholto brings Indian servants back to England with him; Tonga is from the Andaman Islands.

How are working Londoners presented?

Conan Doyle depicts the lower class of Londoners as working men and women who speak 'common', drop their aitches and use everyday idioms. Examples are when Watson fetches the dog Toby from Mr Sherman in Lambeth (Chapter 7); Holmes talks to Mrs Smith (Chapter 8), McMurdo (Chapter 2), and Wiggins (Chapter 8). Though clearly from a different class to Holmes, these characters do seem to trust Holmes.

Key Quotations to Learn

Mud-coloured clouds drooped sadly over the muddy streets. (Chapter 3)

[The] monster tentacles which the giant city was throwing out into the country. (Chapter 3)

There was something strangely incongruous in this Oriental figure framed in the commonplace doorway of a third-rate suburban dwelling-house. (Chapter 3)

Summary

- *The Sign of the Four* is a **contemporary novel**.
- London streets are overcrowded, dirty and depressing; the suburbs are threatening, alien and hideous.
- The lower class is presented as uneducated and blunt but colourful.
- Several characters from other cultures indicate London's increasingly multicultural population.

Sample Analysis

When Watson describes the crowded Strand he uses **pathetic fallacy**, connecting the dismal scene with his own unease. He finds 'something eerie and ghostlike in the endless procession of faces' and the **adjectives** 'eerie' and 'ghostlike' suggest there is something sinister, frightening and inhuman about the faces. This is emphasised by 'endless' – never ending, too many to count – and 'procession' indicating a ceremonial, orderly movement lacking spontaneity. It's a description that shows Watson's horrified reaction to the deadening effects of the city on human life.

Questions

QUICK TEST
1. What is Watson's reaction to the scene on the Strand?
2. How does he describe the suburbs?
3. Give two examples of characters from non-British cultures.
4. Give two examples of lower-class, working Londoners.
5. How do lower-class people generally respond to Holmes?

EXAM PRACTICE
Using one or more of the 'Key Quotations to Learn', write a paragraph analysing Conan Doyle's presentation of London.

Police and Criminals

You must be able to: understand how Conan Doyle presents attitudes to police and criminality in the novel.

What were late-Victorian attitudes to criminals and the police?

In 1888, there was extensive newspaper coverage of murders committed by the serial killer 'Jack the Ripper' in the East End of London. Despite substantial efforts, detectives were unable to capture the killer. Violence sold newspapers, and readers were frightened yet fascinated by the sensational reports. Other types of crime included theft, embezzlement, pickpocketing and prostitution.

Crime, particularly in London and concentrated around the dockyards, was a growing problem in the Victorian period. Crimes were often violent. Drunkenness and drug use was widespread (chiefly opium and cocaine, both readily available without prescription). A rise in crime was a natural consequence of great poverty alongside London's growing trade and affluence, plus the rapidly rising population.

Robert Peel had set up the first professional police force to protect Londoners in 1829. They were known as 'Peelers' but the quality of the first policemen was poor and they were not immediately popular. By the 1880s, a national police force had been established, subject to government audit and regulation, and standards had improved. However, the **stereotype** of the 'Peeler' as stupid, inept and common continued, and London remained a dangerous place to live.

Conan Doyle presents the police in a way that mirrors this middle-class readership's view of the police. Although Athelney Jones is affable, he is also pompous and stupid.

How are criminals presented?

Victorians were fascinated by the criminal mind. They believed a so-called 'criminal class' of people (who were from the lower class and therefore uneducated) were responsible for most crime, especially violence and theft. Victorians believed in the **pseudo-science** of **physiognomy**: the assessment of character or personality from the physical appearance of a person's body, especially the face. Therefore, to Victorians, if a person looked like a criminal, then he or she probably was.

To solve this crime, Holmes puts himself in the criminal's mind. In Chapter 10 he explains how he had to think like Small, a man of 'low cunning' and incapable of 'delicate finesse'. Small must lack education, because he is a member of the criminal class. That is Holmes's assumption, a very common idea of the time. But later, he admits to Watson, 'this man Small is a pretty shrewd fellow'.

Key Quotations to Learn

'But here are the regulars, so the auxiliary forces may beat a retreat.' (Holmes: Chapter 6)

'The energetic Jones ...' (Holmes: Chapter 8)

'It is the unofficial force – the Baker Street irregulars.' (Holmes: Chapter 8)

Summary

- The official detective force is presented as bumbling and humorously inept.
- Police are presented as useful for arresting criminals but not for solving crimes.
- News reports were often sensationalist.
- Victorians thought that a person's character (such as criminality) could be observed in their facial features.
- Holmes tried to think like a criminal in order to solve the case.

Sample Analysis

Conan Doyle uses physiognomy when he describes the criminal Small's 'wild cruel eyes and an expression of concentrated malevolence' – 'cruel' and 'malevolent' are **synonyms** for evil, and 'wild' conveys how Small's passions make him uncivilised. He does not fit into civilised society; 'concentrated' emphasises the strength and power of his will to do evil. All of this can be clearly seen on Small's face.

Questions

QUICK TEST
1. Which true crime case made big news in 1888?
2. What contributed to the rapid rise in crime during the Victorian period?
3. When was the first London Metropolitan Police force set up?
4. What were 'Peelers'?
5. What is physiognomy?

EXAM PRACTICE
Using one or more of the 'Key Quotations to Learn', analyse how Conan Doyle highlights aspects of law enforcement in the novel.

Empire

You must be able to: understand how Victorian ideas about Empire are presented in the novel.

What did the British Empire mean to late Victorians?

By 1888, the British Empire was almost at full reach and Britain was the foremost global power. Key countries in the Empire included India, Canada, Australia, New Zealand and South Africa.

For Victorians, the Empire **symbolised** wealth and power. Military power over indigenous (native) populations had to be maintained. They absolutely believed in the supremacy of British rule and values, culture and education.

Victorians were fascinated and intrigued by non-white people, but also feared and distrusted them for being **Other**: they assumed them to be savage, uncivilised, immoral and violent.

Originally the British went to India to trade not rule but gradually the relationship changed. The British exploited India, making and taking huge fortunes from local princes. Tensions came to a head in the Indian Rebellion of 1857, a serious challenge which the British military finally put down. In 1858, responsibility for governing India was formally passed to parliament and the British crown. Queen Victoria was made Empress of India in 1876.

How is Empire presented in the novel?

Empire is an important backdrop. Many characters are connected to the Empire's activities. Dr Watson is an ex-army surgeon injured in Afghanistan 'adventures'; Morstan and Sholto were high-ranking Indian Army officers. Small lost his leg while serving in the Indian Army. He witnessed the Indian Rebellion first-hand: first when working on a plantation near Agra, then defending Agra Fort.

Sholto brings an Indian servant, Lal Rao, to England with him. Thaddeus has a Hindoo house servant.

The Agra treasure, which belonged to an Indian rajah, is symbolic of **imperialist** attitudes towards foreign wealth – it was something that could be simply stolen, for personal gain.

Small's treatment of Tonga is typically imperialist. He exploits Tonga's loyalty. He makes money by exhibiting him as a freak. He is violent ('welted the little devil with the slack end of a rope'). Yet, Tonga was 'staunch and true' and was more loyal to Small than the Englishmen Sholto and Morstan were.

Watson's reaction to Tonga – 'an unhallowed dwarf with his hideous face, and his strong yellow teeth gnashing' – is typically Victorian: Tonga is a savage, terrifying, violent, and armed with poisoned darts. Just as the British defended Agra against the 'black devils', Watson and Holmes defend themselves against the Islander's dart, but with bullets.

Key Quotations to Learn

'[By] taking the Queen's shilling and joining the Third Buffs, which was just starting for India.' (Small: Chapter 12)

'[There] were two hundred thousand black devils let loose and the country was a perfect hell.' (Small: Chapter 12)

'We earned a living at this time by exhibiting my poor Tonga at fairs and other such places as the black cannibal.' (Small: Chapter 12)

Summary

- British military rule in India is an important context in the story.
- The British Empire in the Victorian era is an important backdrop.
- Watson views Tonga as barely human.
- Small's treatment of Tonga is typical of Victorian beliefs about Empire.

Sample Analysis

Conan Doyle presents the Victorian attitude that the Empire was a source of wealth and exotic pleasures. He describes how, in Thaddeus' apartment, 'two great tiger-skins thrown athwart it increased the suggestion of Eastern luxury'. The **image** of tigers hunted and killed for their skins, then brought to England as decorative trophies is carefully chosen. It is symbolic of how the Victorians plundered resources from countries in the Empire, and how these treasures then became status symbols of the owner's wealth and power, as indicated by the **phrase** 'Eastern luxury'.

Questions

QUICK TEST
1. How did Victorians view people from other cultures?
2. What happened the year after the Indian Rebellion?
3. Name two characters who served as Indian Army officers.
4. Where was Small working in 1857?
5. How did Small use Tonga to make a living?

EXAM PRACTICE
Using one or more of the 'Key Quotations to Learn', write a paragraph analysing aspects of Victorian British Empire as presented in the novel.

You must be able to: understand the literary context of the novel and how it influenced its writing.

Why were detective novels popular?

Rising crime in overcrowded towns and Victorian fascination with criminals and detection created an appetite for crime novels. The genre was characterised by lurid details intended to thrill its audience. Wilkie Collins' *The Moonstone*, with its detective Sergeant Cuff, is widely regarded as establishing the detective fiction genre. A rash of detective fiction stories followed during the 1870s–80s and they were enormously popular. They were **potboilers**, often involving plot resolutions that relied on unlikely coincidences or information suddenly coming to light. The genre is responsible for creating the fictional detective – a figure that retains enormous popularity today. Another key element of the Victorian crime novel is that the criminal is always caught, and order restored.

What was different about Conan Doyle's story?

Conan Doyle used the key features of this relatively new fiction genre, but he also introduced several new elements. His plots are always logical, with everything having a rational explanation. In showing Holmes at work, Conan Doyle presents the 'science' of criminal detection: forensic, evidence-based, credible and realistic. Conan Doyle makes readers privy to all information known to Watson, Holmes's loyal accomplice. This involves readers in the detective process.

Also new was the use of criminal profiling: Holmes puts himself in Small's shoes. Other innovations are the way Holmes's methods combine the scientific (such as handwriting analysis of Mary's letter) with probability – as when he guesses which way the *Aurora* will go when it leaves the dock, 'It is certainly ten to one that they go downstream'.

What other literary genre influenced Conan Doyle?

Conan Doyle admired **Gothic** fiction writer Edgar Allen Poe, and the Gothic influence can be seen in the horrifying description of Bartholomew's corpse with its 'horrible smile, a fixed and unnatural grin' and the image of Small's face looking in 'out of the darkness' through Morstan's window.

Key Quotations to Learn

'He possesses two out of the three qualities necessary for the ideal detective.' (Holmes: Chapter 1)

'You have an extraordinary genius for minutiae.' (Watson: Chapter 1)

'He came through the hole in the roof,' I cried. (Watson: Chapter 6)

'It will be clear enough to you soon.' (Holmes: Chapter 6)

Summary

- At this time, detective fiction was a new genre but very popular.
- Holmes's methods can be traced to those of earlier fictional detectives.
- Conan Doyle's careful plotting, choice of narrator and characterisation of police detectives were important innovations.

Sample Analysis

In Sherlock Holmes, Conan Doyle created a detective unlike any who came before. Rather than using unlikely coincidence to solve a case, Holmes uses forensic techniques, evidence analysis, procedures and statistical hypotheses. He approaches the case as a scientist, 'it confirms my diagnosis, as you doctors express it.' His use of the scientific words 'confirm' and 'diagnosis' in the context of crime detection shows he thinks of himself as a scientist who analyses facts. This attitude is reinforced by his reference to 'you doctors' (that is, Watson) showing that Holmes feels he is speaking as one man of science to another.

Questions

QUICK TEST

1. Why were crime novels popular in the late 19th century?
2. Why did crime writers include lurid details of crimes?
3. Which key literary character type was a feature of crime novels?
4. What is different about Conan Doyle's plots?
5. Which other popular literary genre influenced Conan Doyle?

EXAM PRACTICE

Using one or more of the 'Key Quotations to Learn', write a paragraph analysing how Conan Doyle uses elements of detective fiction in the novel.

Class

You must be able to: understand how ideas about class are presented in the novel.

What did 'class' mean to Victorians?

Victorian society was segmented into classes of people – upper (titled aristocracy), wealthy, educated middle (professions and businessmen) and lower (ordinary, uneducated working people). This was not something that the **Establishment** (those with vested interests in maintaining their money, status, power and influence) wanted to change.

But by the end of the century, things *were* changing. Travel was becoming easier and cheaper. Newspapers and books became more affordable. More people were becoming educated and wanted to better themselves. Some people started to question **social inequality** and wanted to change the **status quo**.

Interest in **Bohemianism** – a radical, alternative lifestyle involving artistic pursuits that was deliberately **anti-establishment** – was also growing. This made the upper- and middle-classes anxious as they saw it as a challenge to their Victorian values: order, morality, retaining established class difference, and the authority of law.

How is social inequality shown in the novel?

We see how Watson's acute sense of social inequality makes him feel inferior to and unworthy of Mary once he thinks she will inherit vast wealth. His middle-class anxiety about not being good enough tells him wealth would make her unattainable. Thaddeus is an example of an **aesthete**: a person of refined sensibilities, who therefore shuns the common people.

Holmes has a refined sensibility and superior intellect – hallmarks of the educated class. He shows his superior education when he quotes foreign philosophers. He also has elements of the aesthete: he uses cocaine because he is bored by real life; he is condescending towards the lower orders, and considers the police to be lower class, bumbling types (useful for brawn but not for brain work). Unlike the nervy Thaddeus, Holmes mixes easily with the lower orders – they like and respect him, and he is able to get out of them exactly what he wants. We see Holmes's 'common touch' when he gets information about the *Aurora* from Mrs Smith. His exchange with McMurdo is another example.

Conan Doyle presents working Londoners as stereotypes in language, thought and action. They can be deferential (Mrs Smith addresses Holmes as 'Sir') in accordance with class division, but they are also presented as stupid, comical **caricatures**. They often use common slang. For example, Mr Sherman offers to drop a 'wiper' (a metal cam or shaft) on Watson's head, 'if you don't hook it!'

Key Quotations to Learn

'[There] is nothing more unaesthetic than a policeman.' (Thaddeus: Chapter 4)

Might she not look on me as a mere vulgar fortune-seeker? (Watson: Chapter 7)

This Agra treasure intervened like an impassable barrier between us. (Watson: Chapter 7)

Summary

- Class and social inequality were hallmarks of society at this time.
- Changes were starting to disturb the status quo, causing upper and middle-class fear and anxiety.
- A new spirit of artistic Bohemianism challenged conventional Victorian values.

Sample Analysis

When Holmes calls the yard workers 'Dirty looking rascals', he's expressing a middle-class Victorian distaste for the lower classes. They appear 'dirty' – an adjective that means unclean (because dock work is dirty) but also implies immoral (they are dishonest or disreputable). This is reinforced by 'rascals', which also **connotes** dishonesty, though of a harmless, mischievous or playful kind. Holmes's words indicate that though he finds the workers distasteful, and probably dishonest, they are not threatening or evil.

Questions

QUICK TEST
1. How was Victorian society divided?
2. What things were threatening to change the status quo?
3. What were typical Victorian values?
4. Which character is an example of an aesthete?
5. Name one working-class character.

EXAM PRACTICE
Using one or more of the 'Key Quotations to Learn', write a paragraph analysing how Conan Doyle presents attitudes to class division in the novel.

You must be able to: understand how the circumstances in which it was written affect the novel.

How did the novel come to be written?

Conan Doyle was commissioned to write the story for *Lippincott's Magazine* and it was first published in February 1890. *Lippincott's* was one of several popular magazines that were chiefly intended to entertain but also educate readers. Therefore, Conan Doyle's story had to be exciting but also educational and moral. He had published the first Sherlock Holmes story, *A Study in Scarlet*, in 1887, also in a magazine. Even though each story was published complete, Conan Doyle often ended his chapters on **cliffhangers**, a traditional format for stories published in instalments, in this case monthly. Cliffhangers make readers want to read on and are a hallmark of thriller stories.

Why did he choose to set it in London?

Conan Doyle set the novel in contemporary London to create a sense of **verisimilitude**. The London he describes would have been very familiar to his readers, and this sense of authenticity would have made it more exciting. Conan Doyle did not live in London at this time, but his research, especially of the city's geography, was painstaking. He succeeds in creating a sense of what it was like to be in Victorian London – the London fog ('The yellow glare from the shop windows streamed out into the steamy, vaporous air'), the transport ('a street Arab led across a four-wheeler and opened the door'), the wharf ('close to the rude landing-stage was a small brick house'), London at night ('the last rays of the sun were gilding the cross upon the summit of St Paul's), and the geography of south London ('Rochester Row ... Now Vincent Square. Now we come out on the Vauxhall Bridge Road').

How did Conan Doyle's background influence the novel?

Conan Doyle was a general practitioner and his medical training clearly influences the novel. His decision to make Watson a doctor is an obvious connection, as is the way he uses Watson's medical knowledge, for example when he identifies Bartholomew's cause of death 'from some powerful vegetable alkaloid'. It is also evident in the language Holmes uses to describe his occupation – a 'consulting detective' – and in the scientific language in which he and Watson discuss the 'case' (another medical **term**): 'hypothesis', 'diagnosis', 'demonstration'.

Key Quotations to Learn

'Show them in to me, *khitmutgar*,' it said. 'Show them straight in to me.' (Thaddeus: Chapter 3)

'You know my methods. Apply them, and it will be instructive to compare results.' (Holmes: Chapter 6)

'It is the only hypothesis which covers the facts.' (Holmes: Chapter 7)

'Now, do consider the data. Diminutive footmarks, toes never fettered by boots ... What do you make of all this?' (Holmes: Chapter 8)

Summary

- Conan Doyle often uses cliffhangers to end chapters, to create suspense and excitement.
- His medical background is seen in his choice of Dr Watson as narrator, and in Holmes's scientific approach to detection.
- He set the story in contemporary London to build **plausibility**, so that readers would readily relate to it.

Sample Analysis

Conan Doyle calls Chapter 1 'The Science of Deduction': although 'science' is an **abstract noun**, the use of the **definite article** 'the' gives the phrase a sense of particularity and seriousness. The **formal register** of 'deduction' adds to the tone of grandeur, indicating that the writer intends to seriously examine this particular branch of scientific enquiry: detective work. These language choices suggest that the chapter will have the flavour of academic treatise, intended to educate as well as being a story intended to entertain.

Questions

QUICK TEST
1. Where was the story first published?
2. Which **literary device**, associated with serial publishing, does Conan Doyle use to create narrative suspense?
3. Why did he choose to set the novel in contemporary London?
4. Which character has the same profession as Conan Doyle?

EXAM PRACTICE
Using one or more of the 'Key Quotations to Learn', write a paragraph explaining how Conan Doyle's own background influenced the novel.

You must be able to: analyse how Holmes is presented in the novel.

What makes Holmes a genius detective?

Holmes finds the 'dull routine of existence' almost unbearable. He needs the challenge of a case to give him 'mental exaltation'. When on a case, Holmes becomes obsessed with solving it and exhibits inexhaustible energy. When not solving a crime, lethargy and boredom consume him, and he self-medicates by taking opiates (legally available at this time).

Holmes is observant, methodical and has an extraordinary depth of knowledge on a variety of arcane (mysterious) subjects. He has a powerfully brilliant, deductive mind and remarkable research skills, but he is also prepared to persevere with hard and boring tasks, such as when he visits fifteen boatyards before finding the *Aurora*. He is a master of disguise. When it is in his interest, he possesses an uncanny ability to get what he needs out of people, whatever their background.

Holmes does not get emotionally involved in any situation; this **objectivity** is an advantage to the detective. To him, crimes are problems to be solved, people are units, and their actions, on average, are predictable.

What is Holmes like as a person?

Holmes can be cold and unemotional, vain and arrogant. He lacks social grace, can be insensitive to others' feelings and is **sarcastic** to those who are less brilliant than him (everyone else). He has a sense of humour: he and Watson laugh when Toby tracks down a barrel of creosote; he enjoys a news report that exaggerates Jones's skills and he is delighted when his disguise fools Jones and Watson.

Holmes's lack of empathy makes him calculating, demanding and controlling. He is an accomplished violinist; his musicianship is one of the few ways he expresses emotion.

How does Watson view Holmes?

Watson admires and respects his friend's 'masterly manner' but is not blind to his faults: he advises Holmes to stop using cocaine, and he cringes at Holmes's abrupt manner with Mary. Holmes regards Watson as a friend and clearly has affection for him, but he treats Watson as a rather dim pupil or as merely a loyal servant, for example, when Holmes instructs Watson to fetch the dog Toby. Watson accepts this relationship. He knows that he is 'ordinary' compared to his exceptionally brilliant friend.

Key Quotations to Learn

'Give me problems, give me work, give me the most **abstruse** cryptogram ...' (Holmes: Chapter 1)

'Pray accept my apologies, viewing the matter as an abstract problem, I had forgotten how personal and painful a thing it might be to you.' (Holmes: Chapter 1)

'Detection is, or ought to be, an exact science, and should be treated in the same cold and unemotional manner.' (Holmes: Chapter 1)

Summary

- Watson presents Holmes as a genius detective but a flawed human.
- On a case, Holmes is a workaholic; when he has no case, boredom drives him to take opiates.
- He is cold, unemotional, and focuses on facts, which is an advantage in solving crimes.

Sample Analysis

Conan Doyle uses animal **imagery** to describe Holmes when he is examining a crime scene. Holmes's movements are 'like those of a trained blood-hound picking out a scent'. Bloodhounds persistently follow a scent and so this **simile** suggests that detective work is instinctive to Holmes. The adjective 'trained' indicates the level of skill and careful understanding that he applies to the task.

Questions

QUICK TEST
1. How does Holmes find relief from the boredom of ordinary life?
2. How does being unemotional help him to solve cases?
3. Name one way he expresses his emotions.
4. What does Watson admire about Holmes?
5. Give an example of how Holmes treats Watson as a loyal servant.

EXAM PRACTICE
Using one or more of the 'Key Quotations to Learn', write a paragraph analysing how Conan Doyle presents Holmes as cold and unemotional.

Sherlock Holmes II

You must be able to: analyse how Holmes is presented in the novel.

How are the many facets of Holmes's character presented?

He is man whose 'nimble and speculative' mind, and mindset, is different to everyone else's. Sometimes Conan Doyle puts him in the role of teacher with Watson as pupil. This fulfils a structural purpose for Conan Doyle, because, as narrator, Watson needs to convey important facts about the case to the reader. This is also why Watson often questions Holmes. Holmes is an authority and an expert and (annoyingly for Jones) is always right. Jones calls him 'Mr Theorist' in a sneering way, but this is because he is jealous of Holmes.

Conan Doyle presents Holmes as a complex and often contradictory character. He is often serious, but he has a sense of humour. He's a scientist who likes to classify, connect and find answers, yet he takes cocaine despite knowing it is bad for him. Watson calls his friend 'brilliant' and says that 'when he chose', Holmes could be good company. Yet, Holmes can be 'morose' and distant, even with Watson, when things aren't going well – as for example when they are waiting for news of the *Aurora*. Holmes writes highly technical monographs (detailed studies) on obscure subjects like types of tobacco ash, and he quotes foreign phrases from memory (further evidence of his brilliance) yet he can easily talk to ordinary people when he wants information from them.

Holmes admits he has a dual personality when he says, 'there are in me the makings of a very fine loafer and also of a pretty spry sort of fellow.'

Is Holmes likeable?

Conan Doyle presents several elements in Holmes's character that are less appealing to the modern reader. He can be manipulative (as when he 'strategically' addresses little Jack Smith as 'Dear little chap!' because he wants information from Jack's mother), and he is dismissive of people who are intellectually inferior to him. For example, he says of the workers in Jacobson's Yard, 'Dirty-looking rascals, but I suppose everyone has some little immortal spark concealed about him'. He also thinks women 'are never entirely to be trusted'. Conan Doyle presents Holmes as an intellectual snob whose immense intellect sometimes prevents him from expressing human feelings. This is why his affection for Watson ('my dear fellow', 'my dear doctor') is so important: it humanises Holmes.

Does Holmes develop as a character?

Conan Doyle ends the novel as he began it, with Holmes reaching for cocaine. Watson points out that Jones has got the credit, Watson has got a wife, but even though Holmes 'has done all the work', he has got nothing at all – suggesting that Holmes has not developed or changed.

Key Quotations to Learn

'See how that one little cloud floats like a pink feather from some gigantic flamingo.' (Holmes: Chapter 7)

'I never remember feeling tired by work, though idleness exhausts me completely.' (Holmes: Chapter 8)

'Whatever is emotional is opposed to that true cold reason which I place above all things.' (Holmes: Chapter 12)

Summary

- Conan Doyle presents Holmes as a complex and often contradictory character.
- He's a **polymath**, violinist, philosopher, scientist, writer, teacher, guru, friend ... and more.
- Conan Doyle does not present Holmes as an **idealised** character; his character has unattractive aspects.

Sample Analysis

Conan Doyle presents Holmes as a teacher. He shows how Holmes chides Watson, '"You will not apply my precepts," he said, shaking his head.' The word 'precepts' carries **connotations** of religious rules, emphasising Holmes's (somewhat arrogant) view that Watson is Holmes's pupil or disciple, with Holmes in the role of guru.

Questions

QUICK TEST
1. Why is it important to the structure of the novel that Watson is in the role of pupil?
2. What name does Jones give Holmes?
3. What kind of publications does Holmes write?
4. Which two contradictory aspects of his own personality does Holmes identify?
5. Why does Conan Doyle choose to end the novel as he began it?

EXAM PRACTICE
Using one or more of the 'Key Quotations to Learn', write a paragraph analysing how Conan Doyle presents Holmes as a complex and contradictory character.

Dr Watson I

You must be able to: analyse how Watson is presented in the novel.

What makes Watson useful as a narrator?

Using Watson as narrator enables Conan Doyle to show Holmes at work from a close perspective. As narrator, Watson filters information to the reader: everything we know about Holmes and the case, we know through Watson. The reader trusts Watson's account because he is a responsible, middle-class, retired army doctor.

What is Watson like as a person?

He is good-natured, sensitive, and wants to help people. He is willing to fill awkward silences in social situations, often because he feels a need to cover for Holmes's silence – for example, when the three ride in the cab to the Lyceum Theatre. He is loyal and principled, determined that Mary should get the treasure even if helping her do so will hurt his chances with her.

Watson's love for Mary shows his affectionate and romantic nature. When he thinks Mary is an heiress to a great fortune, Watson reveals his concerns about their unequal social status – he thinks he won't be good enough or have a chance of being accepted by Mary if she is rich. This also shows he has quite a poor self-image.

In what ways is he a contrast to Holmes?

Conan Doyle uses Watson as a **foil** for Holmes's genius and lack of emotion. Watson is softer and more caring than Holmes, providing a contrast to his friend's cold brilliance. Watson is an educated man of science but he looks stupid when compared to Holmes. However, compared to Watson, Holmes seems cold and unfeeling. Holmes's arrogant superiority sometimes irritates Watson, for example, when, in Chapter 1, Holmes criticises Watson for romanticising his last case in a story for a magazine. When Watson tells Holmes he's to marry Mary, Holmes groans. When Watson asks Holmes to comment on Mary's 'attractive' appearance, Holmes replies 'a client to me is a mere unit, a factor in a problem'. These examples indicate the difference between the two men. Watson is all heart; Holmes is all head.

Key Quotations to Learn

What was I, an army surgeon with a weak leg and a weaker banking account, that I should dare to think of such things? (Chapter 2)

'They appear to be much as other footmarks.' 'Not at all. Look here!' (Watson and Holmes: Chapter 7)

'You will not apply my precept,' he said, shaking his head. (Chapter 6)

Summary

- Watson is a first-person narrator and he is Holmes's assistant, giving us a unique and privileged view of the detective.
- Conan Doyle presents Watson as responsible and principled to build his credibility as narrator.
- Watson is a foil for Holmes.

Sample Analysis

Watson is in touch with his own emotions and his language is occasionally **cliched** and sentimental. When he and Mary hold hands 'like two children' in the grounds at Pondicherry Lodge he comments that 'there was peace in our hearts for all the dark things that surrounded us'. His use of **metonymy**, with 'hearts' representing their shared love, is a romantic cliché, but the word 'peace' shows that they have shared strength against the 'dark things' that surround them. The 'dark things' are both **literal** (the mounds of dirt and the night's darkness) and **metaphorical** (their unspoken fears that there is evil here).

Questions

QUICK TEST
1. What does using Watson as narrator enable Conan Doyle to do?
2. Who does Watson fall in love with?
3. Why does Watson feel he will have no chance with her?
4. Why is Holmes unhappy with Watson's magazine story?
5. What aspect of Holmes's character sometimes irritates Watson?

EXAM PRACTICE
Using one or more of the 'Key Quotations to Learn', write a paragraph analysing how Conan Doyle presents Watson as a foil for Holmes.

You must be able to: analyse how Dr Watson is presented in the novel.

How does Conan Doyle use Watson as the moral centre of the novel?

Conan Doyle uses Watson's strong sense of morality as a **touchstone**. He uses Watson's good character to represent the solid, middle-class, Victorian values of morality, society, class and wealth. He is absolutely certain that he knows what is 'good/right' and 'evil/wrong' when he sees it, and through him, readers are able to evaluate good and evil forces in the novel.

For example, Watson is tormented that he is not good enough for Mary, even before he learns that she's an heiress. The treasure puts Mary further out of his reach, which reveal his typically middle-class Victorian attitudes about class. Once the treasure is lost, he berates himself, 'It was selfish, no doubt, disloyal, wrong' because he feels happy that 'the golden barrier was gone between us'. Again this shows Watson has an acute certainty about right and wrong.

When Watson feels disgust, as when he hears how Small conspired to kill the merchant Achmet, Conan Doyle intends the reader to feel it too. When Watson feels horror, as when he sees Tonga's 'hideous face' 'marked with all bestiality and cruelty' on the *Aurora*, readers feel the same.

How does Conan Doyle use Watson to examine Holmes?

Watson's admiration for Holmes is not outright hero worship and nor is it blinkered. He sometimes questions and challenges his friend. For example, Watson advises Holmes not to take cocaine (it might damage his mind); he asks Holmes to justify his hypothesis about Small; he tests him with his brother's watch; when Holmes says women 'are never to be trusted', Watson notes that this is an 'atrocious sentiment'.

This critical distance between Watson and Holmes is important as it enables Conan Doyle to emphasise the eccentric genius of Holmes (we don't always know what he's thinking or what he's doing, any more than Watson does), and to see his faults. At the same time, it humanises Watson, because he is prey to doubts and anxieties about his friend.

There is a significant moment when Watson briefly considers of Holmes, 'might he not be suffering from some huge self-deception?' Although brief, this gives us a different view of Holmes and makes us realise that being Holmes's friend is far from easy.

Key Quotations to Learn

'You really are an automaton ... there is something positively inhuman in you at times.' (Watson: Chapter 2)

I could not but think what a terrible criminal he would have made. (Chapter 6)

Could there be, I wondered, some radical flaw in my companion's reasoning? (Chapter 9)

Summary

- Conan Doyle uses Watson to give readers a moral compass, so we know what is good and what is evil.
- Conan Doyle presents Watson as Holmes's critical friend: loyal and true, yet able to see his faults and to challenge him sometimes.

Sample Analysis

Watson describes how he takes out his pistol when he sees Tonga, the 'savage, distorted creature'. Watson's choice of adjectives is significant and here he expresses the Victorian belief that other races were horrifying, dangerous and inferior. 'Savage' means violent but also, uncivilised, primitive and immoral. 'Distorted' means deformed and implies that Tonga is ugly and abnormal. That he is less than human is emphasised by Watson's use of the word 'creature' – a non-human animal.

Questions

QUICK TEST
1. In what way does Watson typify Victorian values?
2. Why does Watson feel 'disloyal' when they discover the treasure is lost?
3. Give one example of Watson correctly identifying evil.
4. Why does Watson challenge Holmes about using cocaine?
5. Why does Conan Doyle present Watson as Holmes's critical friend?

EXAM PRACTICE
Using one or more of the 'Key Quotations to Learn', write a paragraph analysing how Conan Doyle presents Watson as a loyal but critical friend to Holmes.

Mary Morstan

You must be able to: analyse how Mary is presented in the novel.

How is Mary presented?

At the start of the novel Mary is presented as a woman 'wronged', seeking help and protection from Holmes. Her visit to Baker Street sets the plot in motion.

In Chapter 9, she comments on Watson's story, 'two knight-errants to the rescue,' She is joking, but in one sense Mary is presented as the traditional figure in a romantic fairy tale: a damsel in distress, an unknowing heiress, an innocent angel, the object of romantic fantasy.

Conan Doyle's characterisation of Mary is idealised. Mary shows intelligence and good sense when she brings the letters for Holmes to examine the handwriting and, later, she remembers to show him the map found in her father's desk. Caring and principled, she shows little interest in becoming 'the richest heiress in England', being more concerned that Thaddeus is released from custody having been falsely accused, than that the treasure is found. Mary is almost too good to be true.

What does Mary tell us about the status of women in Victorian England?

Watson is the narrator and he is in love with Mary, so she is presented from a biased perspective. This explains the idealised picture we have of her. To Watson, she behaves exactly as Victorian women were supposed to, as the weaker sex: she is emotional, likely to faint, in need of support. She is not concerned with wealth and status; she is modest and unassuming.

Apart from seeking Holmes's help in the first place and producing the map, Mary doesn't do anything to move the story forwards. Rather, she is acted upon, first by the letters and pearls sent anonymously, then by the promise of treasure, and finally by Watson when he declares his love. In this regard Mary fits the stereotype of idealised middle-class Victorian women: passive, dependent and subordinate.

Wealth would have given Mary status and independence, but, Watson believes, would have made her unattainable. In a traditional fairy story, the happy ending would be for Mary to be rich but in this case the happier ending is for her not to be, because only then does Watson feel he can propose. Watson sees wealth as a 'golden barrier' between them and, once it is gone, 'Whoever had lost a treasure, I knew that night that I had gained one.'

Key quotations to learn

[Her] lip trembled, her hand quivered, and she showed every sign of intense internal agitation. (Chapter 2)

She was weak and helpless, shaken in mind and nerve. (Chapter 7)

After the angelic fashion of women, she had borne trouble with a calm face ... she first turned faint and then burst into a passion of weeping. (Chapter 7)

Summary

- Mary is presented as a stereotype of the middle-class Victorian woman-as-angel.
- Our impression of her is Watson's perspective, which is idealised because he is in love with her.
- Mary sets the plot in motion and stands to gain if the treasure is recovered but is otherwise passive.
- Holmes recognises Mary's intelligence and that she has a 'decided genius' for their line of work.

Sample Analysis

Watson's attitude toward Mary epitomises the male Victorian view of women as guardians of what is morally superior: women are virtuous and pure, passive and content. We see this in the limited, clichéd and repetitive adjectives he chooses to describe Mary's character and behaviour: 'sweet' (pliant), 'amiable' (friendly), 'modest' (unambitious, unworldly), and 'calm' (lacking aggression). Mary's opposite would be aggressive, ambitious, greedy – attributes that Victorians like Watson associated with men. Watson's linguistic presentation of Mary betrays his tendency to **prescribe** and limit her as a character and as a person. She is his idea of an ideal Victorian woman, contained and constrained by his Victorian world view.

Questions

QUICK TEST
1. How do we know that Mary is not concerned with wealth?
2. Why does Watson present her in an idealised way?
3. In what way does she show intelligence?
4. Why is not having the treasure a happier ending for Watson and Mary?

EXAM PRACTICE
Using one or more of the 'Key Quotations to Learn', write a paragraph analysing how Conan Doyle presents Mary as an idealised stereotype of Victorian womanhood.

Thaddeus Sholto

You must be able to: analyse how Thaddeus is presented in the novel.

What is Thaddeus like as a person?

He is fair and principled, as is shown by his determination (not shared by Bartholomew) that Mary get her share of the treasure. He is also reclusive and frightened of people, particularly the 'rough crowd'. With his high-pitched voice and strange appearance (bald-headed, bristles of red hair, nervous tics and loose, hanging lip), it is clear that wealth has not made him happy – if anything he is its victim, as it has turned him into a terrified nervous wreck.

What is his purpose in the novel?

As the anonymous sender of the pearls to Mary, Thaddeus adds to the mysterious atmosphere at the start. His careful arrangements for conveying her to his home reveal his distrustful nature. His apartment in South London is ostentatiously furnished with Oriental objects, representative of the spoils of Empire, and he is keen to draw attention to them, thinking that they reflect his own refined sensibility. Conan Doyle uses these elements to create an air of intrigue and decadence as he tells his story.

His flashback, which occupies a whole chapter, is vital in understanding the circumstances of the deaths of Morstan and Major Sholto. He gives Sherlock vital clues about the existence of the treasure, and the part played by the wooden-legged man, later revealed to be Jonathan Small.

How is Thaddeus presented?

He's presented as 'the poor little man' and although he is rich, we get the impression that he is vulnerable and innocent, for, as Watson observes, 'he gave the impression of youth'. He is 'a confirmed hypochondriac' (for example, he asks Watson for an impromptu examination of his heart), which indicates that he is self-absorbed but also that he has a deep-seated need to be looked after, as though he is a sick child. The image of him being almost swallowed by a great overcoat and rabbit-skin cap, 'so that no part of him was visible save for his mobile and peaky face', reinforces our sense that Thaddeus' wealth has disempowered, rather than empowered, him. Indeed, when Thaddeus discovers that Bartholomew is dead, Conan Doyle compares his 'twitching, feeble face' to 'the helpless appealing expression of a terrified child'.

Key quotations to learn

He writhed his hands together ... and his features were in a perpetual jerk. (Chapter 4)

'I am a man of somewhat retiring, and I might even say, refined, tastes.' (Thaddeus: Chapter 4)

[His] twitching feeble face peeping out from the great astrakhan collar had the helpless appealing expression of a terrified child. (Chapter 5)

Summary

- Thaddeus is instrumental (functional) to the plot: he sends the pearls and letters to Mary.
- His wealth and protected upbringing have rendered him a reclusive, nervous hypochondriac.
- He is proud of his cultured tastes, and has a sense of responsibility to Mary not shared by his brother.

Sample Analysis

Thaddeus' apartment 'looked as out of place as a diamond of the first water in a setting of brass' and this simile encapsulates the incongruity of the luxury found inside compared with the drabness of the South London setting. Brass is a common metal but a diamond 'of the first water' (of the purest quality) is rare and valuable. Upon entering the richly furnished apartment, Watson is aware that he leaves the ordinary world behind to enter a very different world of exotic luxury. Conan Doyle uses the simile to convey how the story too is taking us from what is drab and ordinary to a world where we will encounter extraordinary and strange events. The diamond also **foreshadows** the Agra treasure, an important symbol in the story to come.

Questions

QUICK TEST
1. Who is Thaddeus' father?
2. What is unusual about Thaddeus' apartment?
3. Why does Thaddeus prefer not to mix with the lower class?
4. Why did Thaddeus send Mary the pearls?

EXAM PRACTICE
Using one or more of the 'Key Quotations to Learn', write a paragraph analysing the presentation of Thaddeus.

Detective Athelney Jones

You must be able to: analyse how Jones is presented in the novel.

What is our first impression of Jones?

Jones's physique contrasts to Holmes's: whereas Holmes is thin and moves swiftly, Jones is 'burly', 'stout' and heavy-footed. Jones speaks 'pompously'; Holmes speaks 'quietly'. The contrast between them is established from the start. The two trade **sarcasm**. Jones calls Holmes 'Mr Theorist', and Holmes refers to Jones as 'the energetic Jones'.

What is his purpose in the novel?

Jones represents the official police force in the novel, but Holmes does not have a high opinion of his skills. When Jones arrives at the scene of the crime, Holmes gently makes fun of him. When Jones tries to demonstrate his powers of deduction, he succeeds in arriving at the wrong conclusion.

Conan Doyle presents the detective as affable but stupid, compared to Holmes's superior intellect. When Holmes needs to find the *Aurora*, he uses the Baker Street irregulars – his 'unofficial force' – not the regular police. This suggests that the police are not useful in detective situations.

Yet later, when Holmes needs force to capture Small and Tonga, he orders Jones to supply 'two staunch men' and a police launch. Holmes's orders are detailed and precise – Holmes assumes command. Jones agrees to Holmes's demands, 'You are the master of the situation,' accepting Holmes's leadership, at least on this occasion.

Why does Conan Doyle contrast Jones and Holmes?

Jones is pompous and over-confident, and his detective skills look simplistic compared to Holmes's careful procedures. His incompetence therefore makes Holmes look even more brilliant. Conan Doyle also has fun with Jones's lack of self-awareness. Because readers are **complicit** in this joke at Jones's expense, it has the effect of making readers feel that they too are cleverer than Jones.

How does Jones's attitude to Holmes change?

Once Jones realises he has arrested the wrong people, his attitude changes. By the time he visits Baker Street he is 'downcast', 'even apologetic' – the air has been knocked out of him. To Watson he acknowledges Holmes's pre-eminence: 'He's a man who is not to be beat'. At this point, he is quite ready to help Holmes to capture the *Aurora*.

However, once they have secured Small, Watson is amused to see that Jones was 'beginning to give himself airs'. From this we understand that Jones's humility is short-lived.

Key quotations to learn

'[Jones] was red-faced, burly and **plethoric** ...' (Chapter 6)

'Don't promise too much, Mr Theorist, don't promise too much!' snapped the detective. (Chapter 6)

'Well, you are master of the situation.' (Jones to Holmes: Chapter 9)

Jones was already beginning to give himself airs on the strength of the capture. (Chapter 11)

Summary

- Jones is presented as a contrast to Holmes.
- He is over-confident and incompetent as a detective.
- His attitude to Holmes is sneering at first but briefly changes to humility when he realises he needs Holmes's help.

Sample Analysis

By the end of the novel, Jones pays Holmes a compliment, 'you are a connoisseur of crime, but duty is duty'. The word 'connoisseur', which **derives** from French, is often used to indicate expertise in fine art or rare wine. By choosing this word, Jones acknowledges that, when it comes to crime, Holmes has pre-eminent expertise, refined tastes and a level of appreciation that is rare and valuable. Yet, the **alliteration** of 'c' in the phrase 'connoisseur of crime' makes the **epithet** sound slightly sneering – it is a back-handed compliment. He follows this with another alliterative phrase, 'duty is duty', which indicates his pomposity. The **parallelism** of the sentence neatly encapsulates Jones's view that though Holmes has pre-eminent detective skills, unlike Jones, he has no real authority to enforce the law.

Questions

QUICK TEST
1. What does Jones look like?
2. How does he treat Holmes at the start?
3. Why does his attitude change?
4. How does he assist with capturing Small?
5. Has he really changed by the end of the novel?

EXAM PRACTICE
Using one or more of the 'Key Quotations to Learn', write a paragraph analysing Jones's attitude towards Holmes.

Jonathan Small and Tonga

You must be able to: analyse how Jonathan Small and Tonga are presented in the novel.

Why do we need to hear Small's story?

It is important to hear Small's story to confirm that Holmes was completely right. Small's corroboration of Holmes's hypothesis is satisfying for readers. Small's account also gives insight into why he behaved as he did.

How is Small presented?

Our first impression of Small is his malevolent spirit, seen on his terrifying face – with its 'wild cruel eyes' – that scared old Sholto to death. Holmes correctly identifies him by connecting the map, the face, the wooden leg and the fact that he had an unusually small accomplice. These elements add mystery to Small. Where did he come from? Why did he stalk Sholto? Who is he working with? Small is at the heart of the mystery, and to fully answer these questions, Conan Doyle gives Small an extended confession/flashback at the end.

Small's life was one of extraordinary adventures, but it was a difficult life. He is presented as an evil and cruel man, but a survivor. He is hardened by years in prison, driven to criminality by greed and misfortune, and embittered by Sholto's betrayal. His experiences give him a warped sense of justice and morality, 'Where is the justice that I should give it [the treasure] up to those who have never earned it?'

As Holmes observes, Small is 'a pretty shrewd fellow' of 'low cunning'. Sholto lived in fear of Small's cruelty and cleverness: he knew what Small was capable of. His endurance of his many hardships meant that Small believed he had 'earned' the Agra treasure – but it was stolen loot, and he had conspired to murder to obtain it.

How is Tonga presented?

Tonga is a symbol of otherness, darkness and savagery. We never hear Tonga speak – he is merely Small's agent. To Small, he is 'poor Tonga' and 'little Tonga', but also he is 'staunch and true' – showing that Small appreciated that Tonga had a finer side to his nature. To Watson he is a terrifying, evil savage, an 'unhallowed dwarf'. To Holmes, he is a lethal foe. The gazetteer (reference book) Holmes consults describes Andaman natives as 'fierce, morose and intractable' and 'naturally hideous'. The presentation of Tonga exactly fits this stereotype.

Victorian readers probably did not feel much sympathy for Tonga and his fate: he was a dangerous and murdering savage. Modern readers may have more empathy for him.

Key quotations to learn

'[He] was as venomous as a young snake ...' (Small, about Tonga: Chapter 12)

'We earned a living at this time by my exhibiting poor Tonga at fairs ... as the black cannibal.' (Small: Chapter 12)

'He was staunch and true, was little Tonga. No man ever had more faithful a mate.' (Small: Chapter 12)

Summary

- Small is presented as a malevolent spirit from the start.
- He feels wronged by Sholto; this fuels his all-consuming passion for revenge.
- He has a warped sense of morality and justice, thinking the stolen treasure is rightfully his.
- Tonga represents vicious savagery and evil in the novel, yet is also loyal and true to Small.

Sample Analysis

Although Tonga was useful to him, Small says Tonga was 'as venomous as a young snake'. This simile shows that Small knew Tonga had an instinct for violence – he is wild, dangerous and uncontrollable, like a poisonous snake. The use of the adjective 'venomous' is apt because Tonga's lethal weapon is a blow-pipe loaded with poisoned darts. Traditionally, snakes are seen as untrustworthy and so Small here indicates that he never did fully trust Tonga, even though, later, Tonga showed him more loyalty than anyone else.

Questions

QUICK TEST
1. Why is it important that we hear Small's story?
2. Why did Small believe he had 'earned' the treasure?
3. In what ways did he show a warped sense of justice and morality?
4. In what way is the presentation of Tonga a stereotype?

EXAM PRACTICE
Using one or more of the 'Key Quotations to Learn', write a paragraph analysing what his relationship with Tonga tells us about Small.

Detective Skills

You must be able to: analyse how the detective skills of observation and deduction are presented in the novel.

What is deduction and why is observation important?

Deduction is the ability make connections between known facts and reach conclusions. Meticulous observation of minute data is crucial before logical deductions can be made. Holmes possesses great powers of observation and deduction; these, combined with his extensive knowledge, make him a great 'unofficial consulting detective'.

How are they presented in the novel?

The first chapter is called 'The Science of Deduction', and contains two demonstrations of Holmes's skills of observation and deduction. First, Holmes deduces that Watson sent a telegram that morning; then he deduces facts about Watson's brother.

Examples of Holmes's great powers of observation – his 'extraordinary genius for minutiae' – include:

- from close examination of Mary's treasure map, Holmes deduces that it is 'paper of native Indian manufacture'
- as they approach Bartholomew's room, Watson gives a detailed account of how Holmes 'walked slowly from step to step, holding the lamp low, and shooting keen glances'
- the 'impression of a wooden stump' tells Holmes that a wooden-legged man broke into the attic
- the entry point of the poisoned dart tells Holmes the direction it was fired from.

Calling Chapter 6 'Sherlock Holmes Gives a Demonstration', illustrating Holmes's detective methods, gives prominence to the science of detection as a theme.

Holmes uses the Baker Street irregulars to discover things that he thinks the official police force are too inept to find out. This is emphasised by Jones's comically clumsy detective skills.

How does Holmes use deduction?

Holmes analyses facts to reach his conclusions. He gets impatient when Watson does not use the same methods, saying 'try a little analysis yourself'. Applying logic and reason leads Holmes to the truth of the case, however improbable that truth might seem on the surface.

Sometimes Holmes will play the odds: he cannot be sure that the *Aurora* will go downstream, but thinks it's 'ten to one'. He did not follow Smith because it's 'hundred to one against Smith knowing where they live.' Ten to one is a high probability, but a hundred to one against is very low. Here we see Holmes using his deductive powers, and what he *knows for sure*, to inform his decisions about things he *cannot know for sure*. Sometimes even the great detective needs to make an informed guess.

Key Quotations to Learn

'You have an extraordinary genius for minutiae.' (Watson to Holmes: Chapter 1)

'I never guess. It is a shocking habit – destructive to the logical faculty.' (Holmes: Chapter 1)

'[When] you have eliminated the impossible, whatever remains, *however improbable*, must be the truth?' (Holmes to Watson: Chapter 6)

'It is the unofficial force, – the Baker Street irregulars.' (Holmes: Chapter 8)

Summary

- Detective skills are explored chiefly through Holmes's powers of observation and deduction.
- There are many demonstrations of his detective methods and powers.
- Even when he has to guess, Holmes uses probability to create a working hypothesis based on his own deductions.

Sample Analysis

Watson gives a detailed description of Holmes at work when he 'walked slowly from step to step ... shooting keen glances to left and right' observing all the minute detail as he ascends the stairs. The **adverb** 'slowly' indicates that Holmes's careful observation takes time; 'shooting' conveys speed and direction, which contrasts his slow movement with his fast observation. The adjective 'keen' reinforces the idea that although Holmes moves unhurriedly, his visual power is extremely acute and discerning. The language tells us that Holmes is utterly methodical in his search for clues.

Questions

QUICK TEST
1. How does Holmes demonstrate his powers of deduction in Chapter 1?
2. What does Holmes's observation of a wooden stump print tell him?
3. How do some chapter titles give prominence to Holmes's methods?
4. When does Holmes use probability to predict an outcome?

EXAM PRACTICE
Using one or more of the 'Key Quotations to Learn', write a paragraph analysing how Conan Doyle presents Holmes's detective skills.

Evil and Justice

You must be able to: analyse how evil and justice are explored in the novel.

How is evil presented?

Evil is represented by Small and Tonga. Tonga is presented as the embodiment of evil in appearance as well as deed. Small is presented as an evil force but his is a story of a man who became evil through greed, whereas Tonga's evil is presented as innate to his Andaman nature: 'hideous ... intractable and fierce ...'.

Conan Doyle characterises the evil nature of both characters by describing their appearance, in particular their eyes. Small has 'wild cruel eyes'; Tonga's are 'venomous, menacing'. Compare how Mary's eyes, 'large blue ... spiritual and sympathetic', signify her virtue. Small is a 'sunburned, reckless-eyed fellow'; Tonga is 'the black cannibal', and both have black hair, the colour associated with evil and death (Mary is blonde and white-skinned). This colour symbolism is not sophisticated, but it is effective.

Conan Doyle uses sensory imagery to create a menacing atmosphere at moments of high tension. Pondicherry Lodge at night has a 'blighted, ill-omened look'. Its 'gloom and deathly silence, struck a chill to the heart'. As they approach Bartholomew's bedroom they cast 'long black shadows' and this imagery continues to build an atmosphere of evil and tension until Holmes sees the corpse: 'there is something devilish in this, Watson'.

At the **climax** of the story – the boat chase – Doyle uses visual imagery to build an atmosphere of menace and tension. The action takes place in darkness, traditionally a time of evil. Small has 'something black' (the treasure chest) between his knees with Tonga 'a dark mass' beside him. They finally capture Small in 'a wild and desolate place' and the moon casts an eerie light, adding to the sinister atmosphere.

How is justice presented?

The theme of justice is introduced with Thaddeus' letter to Mary promising that she 'shall have justice'. Mary is presented as a 'wronged woman' and 'justice' is linked to recovery of the treasure.

We see injustice when Thaddeus is wrongly arrested for the murder of Bartholomew.

Mary says it is their 'duty to clear him', showing her keen sense of justice.

We see that Holmes has a sense of justice when he tells Thaddeus he can easily clear him of the murder, and later when he tells Small he can prove that Tonga, not Small, killed Bartholomew.

We see Small's faulty, warped notion of 'justice' when he sneers at Jones, 'a pretty justice!', since Small actually acquired the treasure by conspiring to murder. Small argues that he 'earned' the treasure by serving time as a prisoner.

Key Quotations to Learn

'You are a wronged woman and shall have justice.' (Letter to Mary: Chapter 2)

I had one glimpse of his venomous, menacing eyes amid the white swirl of the waters. (About Tonga: Chapter 11)

'A pretty justice! Whose loot is this, if it is not ours?' (Small: Chapter 12)

 **Summary**

- Conan Doyle links the moral state of a character to their appearance.
- He uses black/white symbolism to indicate goodness and evil in people and places.
- Small expresses an alternative view of justice – the criminal's view.
- Holmes and Watson are on the side of justice; in the end, justice wins.

Sample Analysis

Small justifies his claim to the treasure, 'Whose loot is this if it is not ours?', and his use of a **rhetorical question** shows that he is trying to persuade his audience of his point of view. He refers to the treasure informally as 'loot' (stolen goods), as if to remind the listeners that he knows as well as they do that the treasure was stolen. **Implicit** in this is Small's view that, because the four stole the treasure, it rightly belongs to them.

 Questions

QUICK TEST
1. What is it about Tonga's appearance that characterises him as evil?
2. Why does Conan Doyle choose to set key action points at night?
3. In what way is Mary a 'wronged woman'?
4. What is Small's view of 'justice'?

EXAM PRACTICE
Using one or more of the 'Key Quotations to Learn', write a paragraph analysing how Conan Doyle presents the theme of evil.

Imperialism

You must be able to: analyse how the theme of imperialism is presented in the novel.

What attitudes are linked to imperialism?

The novel presents imperialist attitudes towards some of the territories and peoples in the British Empire in the nineteenth century.

Those territories were viewed as exotic and strange, but also as sources of great wealth, luxury and power for the new rulers. Victorians had a sense of fascination for but also fear of foreign people. Any threat to British rule was quickly stamped out and British authority reasserted.

How are these attitudes presented?

The spoils of Empire are seen in Thaddeus' apartment, which is richly decorated with Eastern treasures. The stolen Agra treasure is symbolic of Eastern wealth to be plundered at will. Small's treatment of Tonga typifies the Imperialist attitude that 'savages' were just another commodity to be exploited.

Threat to British rule is shown by Small's account of the Indian Rebellion of 1857. It was a serious challenge to British authority and for a time the British struggled to regain control. Small's attitude to the Indian rebels is typically imperialist: he calls them 'black fiends', betraying their British rulers by turning on them, noting that 'the worst of it was that these men ... were our own picked troops'.

When foreign people turn up in London, their appearance, in native clothes, is 'strangely incongruous' (the phrase used to describe Thaddeus' Hindoo servant). They do not fit, and they are not accepted or integrated. Holmes and Watson both consider Tonga a 'savage' and he is characterised as such. His footprints are strange, too small for an 'ordinary man'; his poisoned darts and club are from a foreign place; he belongs to a race that is known to be intractable to British rule, and known to be cannibals. The implicit fear/fascination in the characterisation of Tonga encapsulates Victorian imperialist attitudes towards foreign people. Later, Watson's description of Tonga communicates the Victorian fear of people from other races, nationalities and origin 'his thick lips were writhed back from his teeth, which grinned and chattered at us with half animal fury.'

Key Quotations to Learn

'So intractable and fierce are they that all the efforts of the British official have failed to win them over in any degree.' (Holmes, reading from the gazetteer: Chapter 8)

'I made at him with the rope's end and cursed him for a blood-thirsty imp.' (Small, about Tonga: Chapter 12)

Summary

- To Victorians, the Empire is a source of wealth to be plundered.
- Tonga encapsulates the Victorian attitude that people untamed by Empire were savages.
- Small's account of the Indian Rebellion and his treatment of Tonga demonstrate the idea that British authority must be asserted over countries in the Empire.

Sample Analysis

Watson's description of Tonga as 'a little black man – the smallest I have ever seen' – with 'a great, misshapen head and a shock of tangled, dishevelled hair' expresses the Victorian view that people from other races were dangerous simply because they were different. 'Misshapen' tells us that Watson identifies Tonga as abnormal – his head is not shaped like 'ours', and he's abnormally small. His dark skin makes him scary and villain-like. Even his 'shock' of hair (a noun that means hair that stands up on end, but also describes Watson's reaction) is out of control ('tangled' and 'dishevelled'). The implication is that Tonga's nature, like his hair, is wild.

Questions

QUICK TEST
1. What did Victorians feel about foreign people?
2. For the rulers, what was the Empire a source of?
3. In what way is the Agra treasure a symbol of imperialism?
4. What does Small's account of the Indian Rebellion tell us about attitudes to Empire?

EXAM PRACTICE
Using one or more of the 'Key Quotations to Learn', write a paragraph analysing how Conan Doyle presents imperialist attitudes.

Greed and Wealth

You must be able to: analyse how the themes of greed and wealth are explored in the novel.

How is greed linked to the Agra treasure?

The treasure is the central symbol of wealth in the novel, inspiring greed in several characters. The message is that greed is a sin which corrupts men and leads to crime, betrayal, fear and death, whereas absence of greed is a virtue.

How is greed presented?

Conan Doyle presents several characters who are motivated by greed. Their greed is indicated by how each reacts to the treasure (wealth), and the ill consequences of their greed are clearly shown.

Thaddeus describes his father, Sholto, as a wealthy man who lived in fear. On his deathbed Sholto confessed that greed caused his troubles. His greed led him to betray his friend Morstan and 'the four'. Because of his greed, Mary was denied her inheritance. Because he argued with Morstan over the treasure, his friend died, and because of all this, he lived in fear that Small would track him down and kill him.

Morstan was also greedy: he wanted the treasure, and his desire for it led ultimately to his death. **Ironically**, he was killed when his head hit the corner of the treasure box.

Bartholomew is portrayed as greedier than his brother. They argued about the treasure, even though both were already wealthy. Bartholomew's greed made him selfish. The idea that greed leads to selfishness is echoed by Small's later comment: 'It is my treasure; and if I can't have the loot I'll take darned good care that no one else does.'

'The four' conspire to steal the treasure, again motivated by greed, with Abdullah Khan saying, 'There will be enough to make every one of us great men and rich chiefs.'

A significant difference between Sholto and Small is that Sholto accepted that his own greed caused his troubles, but Small does not. Small thinks greed is something done to him by the treasure, he doesn't take responsibility for his own greed like Sholto does.

How does Conan Doyle present absence of greed?

Conan Doyle shows how absence of greed is a virtue, and again he does this through attitudes towards the treasure (symbol of wealth). Absence of greed is represented by Mary and by Thaddeus. Mary shows no interest in the treasure. When she learns it is lost, she remains unmoved. Thaddeus says he was not concerned about finding the treasure, as he already had plenty of money.

Key Quotations to Learn

'[So] blind and foolish a thing is avarice.' (Sholto: Chapter 4)

'The cursed greed which has been my besetting sin through life has withheld from her the treasure ...' (Sholto: Chapter 4)

'The treasure is lost,' said Miss Morstan calmly. (Chapter 11)

'[The] Agra treasure, which never brought anything but a curse yet upon the man who owned it.' (Small: Chapter 12)

Summary

- Wealth is symbolised by the Agra treasure.
- Greed is shown to be a sin that corrupts men and destroys human relationships.
- Absence of greed is presented as a virtue.

Sample Analysis

When Sholto reflects on the 'cursed greed which has been my besetting sin through life', he encapsulates an important moral of the story. He uses 'cursed' to show that he knows that greed is the root of his misfortune. The adjective also shows that this knowledge annoys him. A 'besetting sin' is a Biblical phrase and means a fault that someone is prone to. The religious connotation gives the phrase moral significance. The tone is fitting, as it is the start of Sholto's deathbed confession.

Questions

QUICK TEST
1. What does the novel say about the consequences of greed?
2. Which character admits to the sin of greed?
3. Which character blames the treasure for his troubles?
4. How does Conan Doyle link greed, or absence of greed, to the treasure?
5. Which two characters display absence of greed?

EXAM PRACTICE
Using one or more of the 'Key Quotations to Learn', write a paragraph analysing how Conan Doyle explores the causes and consequences of greed.

Fear and Suspense

You must be able to: analyse how Conan Doyle explores aspects of fear and suspense in the novel.

How does Conan Doyle present physical fear?

Conan Doyle uses several characters to present the effects of fear. Thaddeus has 'features in a perpetual jerk', indicating his state of continual terror. Sholto also lived in terror that Small would track him down. When Sholto saw Small at the window, 'his eyes stared wildly, his jaw dropped.' Achmet, the merchant, is the picture of terror: 'his hands twitched as if he had the ague.' Conan Doyle shows that fear is something that weakens people physically.

Conan Doyle's use of Gothic imagery to create terror

Conan Doyle uses Gothic imagery to create a sense of terror and horror for readers. Pondicherry Lodge 'had a blighted, ill-omened look'; Bartholomew's corpse has 'a horrible smile, a fixed and unnatural grin'; Tonga has 'small eyes that glowed and burned with a sombre light'.

What is presented as the antidote to fear and horror?

Holmes's rational, scientific approach provides logic, reason and facts – the natural antidote to fear and horror. Holmes's lack of emotion means that he remains calm in dangerous situations. When Holmes points out Tonga's poisoned dart that just missed them, he simply shrugs his shoulders, whereas Watson feels sick. When they discover Bartholomew, Holmes remarks 'there is something devilish in this', whereas Watson 'recoiled in horror'.

Watson is also presented as an antidote to fear – he is solid, reliable and dependable. He has seen active service in Afghanistan and when Holmes tells him to fire at Tonga, he does so, even though the sight of the little man is terrifying.

How does Conan Doyle create excitement and suspense?

Conan Doyle changes the narrative pace to manage the reader's excitement. Readers cannot be excited all the time, and so he alternates fast-moving, thrilling passages with slower sections in which things are explained but not much happens. The boat chase is one of the thrilling passages; Sholto's death is another.

Slower sections give readers space to process information. They can also be used to build suspense. For example, when Holmes goes off to find the *Aurora*, Watson describes the tension of waiting, 'It was a long day'. Watson's visits to Mary are other lulls in the action, where the focus moves from action to romance.

Sometimes Conan Doyle uses cliffhangers to increase suspense and encourage readers to find out what happens in the next chapter.

Key Quotations to Learn

The features ... were set in a horrible smile, a fixed and unnatural grin. (Chapter 5)

Never did sport give me such a wild thrill as this mad, flying man-hunt down the Thames. (Chapter 10)

'[His] head kept turning to left and right ... like a mouse when he ventures out from his hole.' (Small, about Achmet: Chapter 12)

Summary

- Fear is presented as something that weakens people physically.
- Gothic imagery is used to indicate Watson's horror, and to create it in readers.
- Holmes's rational and logical methods of investigation counteract fear.
- Conan Doyle manages the reader's tension by changing the pace of the narrative.

Sample Analysis

During the chase, Watson describes the sensation of being on the boat, 'With every throb of the engines we sprang and quivered like a living thing'. The word 'throb' conveys the sense that the engines make a rhythmic sound but it also reminds us of the pounding sensation of blood pulsing through a living heart when it beats faster due to physical exertion and exhilaration. He develops the idea that the boat feels as if it is alive with the **verbs** 'sprang' and 'quivered'. He drives the point home in the simile 'like a living thing': it is as if the boat itself is alive and excited.

Questions

QUICK TEST
1. Name one character who shows physical signs of fear.
2. What sort of imagery does Conan Doyle use to inspire horror?
3. How does Holmes's lack of emotion help him?
4. How does the writer use narrative pace to manage suspense and excitement?

EXAM PRACTICE
Using one or more of the 'Key Quotations to Learn', write a paragraph analysing how Conan Doyle presents fear in the novel.

Loyalty and Betrayal

You must be able to: analyse how Conan Doyle presents ideas about loyalty and betrayal in the novel.

How does Conan Doyle present loyalty and betrayal?

The theme of loyalty and betrayal is chiefly presented through the character of Jonathan Small. Loyalty keeps 'the four' together as one group. Small and the three Sikh troopers swore an oath 'to raise no hand and speak no word against us, either now or afterwards.' Small never breaks this oath; he holds fast to it when he could have looked after himself only. It is called into question by Sholto when he asks, 'What have three black fellows to do with our agreement?', to which Small replies, 'they are in with me, and we all go together.'

Small prizes loyalty. He is loyal to the Empire (he volunteers to defend Agra Fort). For him, the worst part of the Indian Rebellion was that the rebels were 'our own picked troops' – that is, they had previously fought *for* the Empire.

Small assumes he can expect the same high level of loyalty from Sholto, a fellow Englishman, and an army man, too. But Sholto betrayed Small. Worse, he betrayed 'the four'. This explains the strength of Small's passion for revenge on Sholto: 'A hundred times I have killed him in my sleep.'

Even though Small's cultural prejudices make him naturally distrustful of Tonga, he acknowledges the Islander's loyalty.

Finally, when Small throws the treasure into the Thames, he acts out of loyalty to 'the four': 'I have acted all through for them as much as for myself. It's been the sign of four with us always.'

Why does Conan Doyle choose to explore loyalty and betrayal through a criminal?

Conan Doyle presents Small as a complex character, despite being a criminal. Previously, fictional criminals tended to be presented as one-dimensional caricatures of evil and menace. Instead, Conan Doyle humanises Small, using him to show that even a criminal is a person with depth and dimension. Small possesses some qualities that are traditionally thought of as positive, such as loyalty. Small's desire for vengeance is evil, yet Conan Doyle's presentation makes it clear that it was Small's very human sense of betrayal that caused it.

In presenting Small as a complex criminal, Conan Doyle emphasises Holmes's brilliance as a detective. Small is a worthy foe and Conan Doyle indicates how psychological profiling is an important aspect of detective work. It is commonly used in police work today, but it was virtually unknown in 1890.

Key Quotations to Learn

'It's been the sign of four with us always.' (Small: Chapter 12)

'The scoundrel had stolen it all.' (Small, about Sholto: Chapter 12)

'He was staunch and true, was little Tonga. No man ever had a more faithful mate.' (Small: Chapter 12)

Summary

- Loyalty and betrayal are presented through Small, who values these things highly.
- Small's sense of betrayal by Sholto is key to understanding his crime.
- Loyalty is a positive trait but Small's strong sense of betrayal fuels his obsession for revenge and results in murder.

Sample Analysis

Interestingly, Small's loyalty to Empire is evident when he says, 'But the Sikh knows the Englishman, and the Englishman knows the Sikh'. He uses singular nouns 'the Sikh' and 'the Englishman' to represent two different groups and he binds them together linguistically through parallelism which perfectly balances the two groups, like an equation. He is saying that both groups 'know' – that is, understand – each other, because of their shared history through Empire. Small's use of the present tense 'knows' gives the statement a sense of timelessness, which indicates for him this is an accepted fact or **truism** rather than opinion.

Questions

QUICK TEST
1. Which group does Small swear an oath of loyalty with?
2. Who betrays Small's trust?
3. What in Small's history shows he has a sense of loyalty to Empire?
4. Which character shows unexpected loyalty to Small?
5. What does Conan Doyle show through his presentation of Small's loyalty?

EXAM PRACTICE
Using one or more of the 'Key Quotations to Learn', write a paragraph analysing Conan Doyle's presentation of loyalty in the novel.

Tips and Assessment Objectives

You must be able to: understand how to approach the exam question and meet the requirements of the mark scheme.

Quick tips

- Read the extract carefully at least twice.

- Make sure you know what the question is asking you. Underline key words and pay particular attention to the bullet point prompts that come with the question.

- You will be expected to show that you understand the novel's characters, themes and context.

- You should spend about 45 minutes on your *The Sign of the Four* response. Allow yourself five minutes to plan your answer so there is some structure to your essay.

- All your paragraphs should contain a clear idea, a relevant reference to the novel (ideally a quotation) and analysis of how Conan Doyle conveys this idea. Whenever possible, you should link your comments to the novel's context.

- It can sometimes help, after each paragraph, to quickly re-read the question to keep yourself focused on the exam task.

- Keep your writing concise. If you waste time 'waffling' you won't be able to include the full range of analysis and understanding that the mark scheme requires.

- It is a good idea to remember what the mark scheme is asking of you.

AO1: Understand and respond to the novel (12 marks)

This is all about coming up with a range of points that match the question, supporting your ideas with references from the novel and writing your essay in a mature, academic style.

Lower	Middle	Upper
The essay has some good ideas that are mostly relevant. Some quotations and references are used to support the ideas.	A clear essay that always focuses on the exam question. Quotations and references support ideas effectively. The response refers to different points in the novel.	A convincing, well-structured essay that answers the question fully. Quotations and references are well chosen and integrated into sentences. The response covers the whole novel (not everything, but ideas from all of the text rather than just focusing on one or two sections).

AO2: Analyse effects of Conan Doyle's language, form and structure (12 marks)

You need to comment on how specific words, language techniques, sentence structures, dialogue or the narrative structure allow Conan Doyle to get his ideas across to the reader. This could simply be something about a character or a larger idea he is exploring through the text. To achieve this, you will need to have learned good quotations to analyse.

Lower	Middle	Upper
Identification of some different methods used by Conan Doyle to convey meaning. Some subject terminology.	Explanation of Conan Doyle's different methods. Clear understanding of the effects of these methods. Accurate use of subject terminology.	Analysis of the full range of Conan Doyle's methods. Thorough exploration of the effects of these methods. Accurate range of subject terminology.

AO3: Understand the relationship between the novel and its context (6 marks)

For this part of the mark scheme, you need to show your understanding of how the characters or Conan Doyle's ideas relate to when he was writing or when the novel was set (both late 19th century).

Lower	Middle	Upper
Some awareness of how ideas in the novel link to its context.	References to relevant aspects of context show a clear understanding.	Exploration is linked to specific aspects of the novel's contexts to show a detailed understanding.

1. Read the following extract from Chapter 11 and then answer the question that follows.

> 'The treasure is lost,' said Miss Morstan, calmly.
>
> As I listened to the words and realised what they meant, a great shadow seemed to pass from my soul. I did not know how this Agra treasure had weighed me down, until now that it was finally removed. It was selfish, no doubt, disloyal, wrong, but I could realise nothing save that the golden barrier was gone from between us.
>
> 'Thank God!' I ejaculated from my very heart.
>
> She looked at me with a quick, questioning smile. 'Why do you say that?' she asked.
>
> 'Because you are within my reach again,' I said, taking her hand. She did not withdraw it. Because I love you, Mary, as truly as ever a man loved a woman. Because this treasure, these riches, sealed my lips. Now that they are gone I can tell you how I love you. That is why I said, "Thank God."'
>
> 'Then I say "Thank God", too,' she whispered, as I drew her to my side. Whoever had lost a treasure, I knew that night that I had gained one.

Starting with this extract, explore how Conan Doyle presents the emotional and romantic side of Dr Watson's character. Write about:

- how Conan Doyle presents the emotional and romantic side of Dr Watson's character in this extract
- how Conan Doyle presents the emotional and romantic side of Dr Watson's character in the novel as a whole.

2. Read the extract from Chapter 1 that begins 'He did not seem offended' and ends 'is my highest reward'.

   Starting with this extract, explore how Conan Doyle presents Holmes as a complex and unusual individual. Write about:

   - how Conan Doyle presents Holmes as a complex and unusual individual in this extract
   - how Conan Doyle presents Holmes as a complex and unusual individual in the novel as a whole.

3. Read the extract from Chapter 7 that begins 'After the angelic fashion' and ends 'shaken in mind and nerve'.

   Starting with this extract, explore how Conan Doyle presents Mary Morstan as a romantic heroine. Write about:

   - how Conan Doyle presents Mary Morstan as a romantic heroine in this extract
   - how Conan Doyle presents Mary Morstan as a romantic heroine in the novel as a whole.

4. Read the extract from Chapter 12 that begins 'He was staunch and true' and ends 'knocked the whole front of his skull in'.

   Starting with this extract, analyse how Conan Doyle presents the character of Jonathan Small. Write about:

   - how Conan Doyle presents the character of Jonathan Small in this extract
   - how Conan Doyle presents the character of Jonathan Small in the novel as a whole.

5. Read the following extract from Chapter 6 and then answer the question that follows.

'You see!' said Athelney Jones, reappearing down the steps again. 'Facts are better than mere theories, after all. My view of the case is confirmed. There is a trap-door communicating with the roof, and it is partly open.'

'It was I who opened it.'

'Oh, indeed! You did notice it, then?' He seemed a little crestfallen at the discovery. 'Well, whoever noticed it, it shows how our gentleman got away. Inspector!'

'Yes, sir,' from the passage.

'Ask Mr Sholto to step this way. Mr Sholto, it is my duty to inform you that anything which you may say will be used against you. I arrest you in the queen's name as being concerned in the death of your brother.'

'There now! Didn't I tell you!' cried the poor little man, throwing out his hands and looking from one to the other of us.

'Don't trouble yourself about it, Mr Sholto,' said Holmes. 'I think I can engage to clear you of the charge.'

'Don't promise too much, Mr Theorist, don't promise too much,' snapped the detective. 'You may find it a harder matter than you think.'

'Not only will I clear him, Mr Jones, but I will make you a present of the name and description of one of the two people who were in this room last night.'

Starting with this extract, explore how Conan Doyle presents crime detection. Write about:
- how Conan Doyle presents crime detection in this extract
- how Conan Doyle presents crime detection in the novel as a whole.

6. Read the extract from Chapter 10 that begins 'We *must* catch her!' and ends 'Get every pound of steam you can'.

   Starting with this extract, explore how Conan Doyle creates a sense of tension and excitement. Write about:

   - how Conan Doyle creates a sense of tension and excitement in this extract

   - how Conan Doyle creates a sense of tension and excitement in the novel as a whole.

7. Read the extract from Chapter 4 that begins 'At this instant a horrible change' and ends 'that wild, fierce face'.

   Starting with this extract, explore how Conan Doyle creates a sense of evil and horror. Write about:

   - how Conan Doyle creates a sense of evil and horror in this extract

   - how Conan Doyle creates a sense of evil and horror in the novel as a whole.

8. Read the extract from Chapter 4 that begins 'We were all astonished' and ends 'subtle and aromatic odour'.

   Starting with this extract, explore how Conan Doyle presents Empire and imperialism. Write about:

   - how Conan Doyle presents Empire and imperialism in this extract

   - how Conan Doyle presents Empire and imperialism in the novel as a whole.

Planning a Character Question Response

You must be able to: understand what an exam question is asking you and prepare your response.

How might an exam question be phrased?

Questions 1–4 are typical character questions. Some may focus on an individual character and some may focus on a relationship. Remember that themes and characters are not mutually exclusive – a character question requires some discussion of themes and a theme question will require discussion of character.

Look again at Question 1 on page 60.

Starting with this extract, explore how Conan Doyle presents the emotional and romantic side of Dr Watson's character. Write about:

- how Conan Doyle presents the emotional and romantic side of Dr Watson's character in this extract

- how Conan Doyle presents the emotional and romantic side of Dr Watson's character in the novel as a whole.

[30 marks]

How do I work out what to do?

The focus of this question is on Dr Watson and his emotional and romantic side. The bullet points remind you that you should divide your answer between the extract and the rest of the novel.

For AO1, you need to show a clear understanding of Dr Watson's emotional and romantic side. You should link this to your understanding of Dr Watson's relationships with Holmes, with Mary Morstan, and of his observations in his role as narrator.

For AO2, 'how' makes it clear you need to analyse the different ways Conan Doyle's use of language, form and structure help to show Dr Watson's emotional and romantic side. You should analyse the extract and include quotations you have learned in your answer.

You also need to link your answer to the context of the novel to achieve your AO3 marks.

How can I plan my essay?

You have approximately 45 minutes to write your essay. This isn't long but you should spend the first five minutes writing a quick plan. This will help you to focus your thoughts and write a well-structured essay.

Try to come up with five or six ideas. Each of these ideas can then be written up as a paragraph in the essay.

You can plan in whatever way you find most useful. Some students like to just make a quick list of points and then renumber them into a logical order. Spider diagrams are particularly popular; look at the example below.

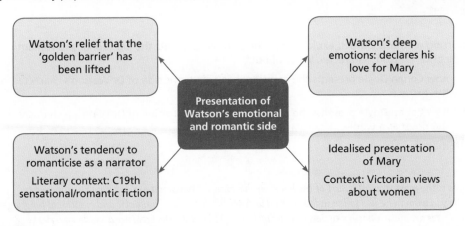

Summary

- Make sure you read the extract and the question carefully so that you know what the focus is.
- Remember to analyse how ideas are conveyed by Conan Doyle.
- Try to relate your ideas to the novel's social and historical context.

Questions

QUICK TEST
1. What key skills do you need to show in your answer?
2. What are the benefits of writing a quick plan for your essay?
3. Why is it better to have learned quotations for the exam?

EXAM PRACTICE
Plan a response to Question 2 on page 60.
Starting with this extract, explore how Conan Doyle presents Holmes as a complex and unusual individual. Write about:
- how Conan Doyle presents Holmes as a complex and unusual individual in this extract
- how Conan Doyle presents Holmes as a complex and unusual individual in the novel as a whole.
[30 marks]

Starting with this extract, explore how Conan Doyle presents the emotional and romantic side of Dr Watson's character. Write about:

- how Conan Doyle presents the emotional and romantic side of Dr Watson's character in this extract
- how Conan Doyle presents the emotional and romantic side of Dr Watson's character in the novel as a whole.

[30 marks]

This is the most romantic part of the book. In this extract, Watson describes how he proposed to Mary, a woman he has fallen in love with. He describes his love in romantic and emotional language and uses dramatic imagery to describe his feelings. (1) He calls the treasure a 'golden barrier', which indicates that the treasure is a symbol. (2) The word 'very' in the phrase 'from my very heart' is emphasised, showing the depth of his feelings. Watson has a very emotional and romantic side, especially when compared with Holmes who can be cold and unemotional. (3)

We can tell the strength of Watson's emotions by the language he uses to talk about his love, such as telling Mary he loves her 'as truly as ever a man loved a woman'. This phrase conveys his sincerity and deep romantic love. (4)

Watson is not embarrassed to talk about his feelings at this point but before this he was cautious of expressing his love because of the treasure. He did not feel worthy of Mary as an heiress to a great fortune. He was worried that he might seem like a fortune hunter. His anxiety shows his sensitivity to social inequality and class. Therefore, when he says, 'I knew that night I had found one', meaning a 'treasure', it is a metaphor for Mary. In other words, now the 'barrier' (the Agra treasure) has gone, Watson has found his own treasure – Mary. (5)

Watson's emotional side is also shown in other parts of the novel. For example, as a narrator he likes to describe scenes and events in an exciting and sensational way and he uses suspense to build interest for readers, so they keep reading the story. The boat chase down the Thames is one example of this and when he describes Bartholomew's dead face with its 'horrible smile and a fixed, unnatural grin' is another. (6) Watson is good at conveying his own feelings of horror, excitement and disgust. For example, when he describes Tonga as 'an unhallowed dwarf with a hideous face' we can tell he feels horror. There are elements of the Gothic fiction tradition, and sensational novels which were popular at the time, in Watson's descriptions. (7)

Watson's presentation of romantic love and of Mary fits with the Victorian stereotype of women as the weaker sex. (8) He has a sentimental view of women and his characterisation of Mary shows this. Mary is gentle, calm and virtuous. She is weak and can be emotional, sometimes tearful and sometimes she faints. Watson feels it is his duty to protect her.

Watson is the narrator and therefore we have real insight into his feelings for Mary at several points in the novel. Conan Doyle also uses Watson's ordinariness and his emotional nature as a foil for Holmes's brilliance and lack of sensitivity. (9)

1. Good use of terminology but lacks example quotation. AO2
2. Limited language analysis. AO2
3. Identification of structure but effect not referenced to author's meaning or intention. AO2
4. Insightful use of quotation and language analysis but not analysed for effect. AO1/AO2
5. Analysis of language and accurate terminology linked to wider theme. AO1/AO2
6. Ideas supported by reference to the whole novel. AO1
7. Explanation of language effects linked to literary context. AO2/AO3
8. Idea related to an understanding of the social context in which the novel was written. AO3
9. Structure identified but effect not analysed. AO1

Questions

EXAM PRACTICE

Choose a paragraph from this essay. Read it through a few times and then try to rewrite it and improve it. You might:

- replace a reference with a quotation or use a better quotation
- ensure quotations are embedded within the sentence
- provide more detailed, or a wider range of, analysis
- use more subject terminology
- link some context to the analysis more effectively.

Starting with this extract, explore how Conan Doyle presents the emotional and romantic side of Dr Watson's character. Write about:

- how Conan Doyle presents the emotional and romantic side of Dr Watson's character in this extract
- how Conan Doyle presents the emotional and romantic side of Dr Watson's character in the novel as a whole.

[30 marks]

Watson is presented as romantic through his feelings towards Mary. (1) Here he declares his love for her, 'as truly as ever a man loved a woman', using a simile to emphasise the sincerity of his feelings. (2)

Conan Doyle presents Watson's love for Mary up to this point through his inner thoughts and feelings, shared with readers. For example, after meeting Mary for the first time, Watson entertains 'dangerous thoughts'. The adjective 'dangerous' implies that his thoughts are sexual and that Watson feels uncomfortable about having them. (3)

Conan Doyle explores the emotional side of Watson's character by showing his anxiety about the difference that the treasure would make to their relationship if Mary inherited it. (4) The extract has the moment when this 'golden barrier' – a metaphor for the treasure which has stood between them – is removed and Watson's intense relief is denoted by his **exclamation**, 'Thank God!' There is a sexual reference in the word 'ejaculated', which means to suddenly cry out but also connotes the sex act. (5) Watson is here presented as a man of intense emotional responses.

Watson is sensitive to social difference and is prey to anxiety about his own self-worth. He's an ex-army surgeon 'with a weak leg and a weaker banking account' – a brutal self-assessment of his comparative physical and financial inadequacy, showing he suffers from a poor self-image. (6) This sensitivity to others' feelings and self-criticism almost prevent Watson from declaring his love for Mary, but by equating wealth with worth, Watson voices accepted notions of Victorian class and society. (7) Mary's wealth would have made her unattainable.

As narrator, Watson tends to romanticise events. This is evident in his poetic use of metaphor in the phrase 'a great shadow seemed to pass from my soul', which conveys how the threat of Mary's inheritance had cast a pall ('shadow') over his spirit ('soul') and forced him to hide his feelings. Now the threat has lifted ('passed'), he is free to express them. (8)

Watson's emotional side is shown by his taste for the sensational and Conan Doyle uses this to build tension and suspense in the novel. There are many examples of this: one is when Watson describes Bartholomew's corpse, using the Gothic imagery of sensational novels that were very popular at this time. (9)

When they drive with Mary through the Strand in Chapter 3, Watson ascribes his own feelings to the scene, using the pathetic fallacy like a Romantic poet. The clouds are 'mud-coloured' and they 'droop sadly' (10) – the appearance of the clouds reflects Watson's depression. This is one example of how Watson has an emotional response to everything he experiences.

Conan Doyle's presentation of Mary denotes Watson's idealised and romantic view of women, and Watson's view of Mary conforms to a Victorian stereotype of women and romantic love. (11) Mary is 'weak and helpless' and though she appears calm, 'after the angelic fashion of women', she later turns faint and weeps passionately. This attitude to women as 'angels' but the weaker, helpless and hopelessly emotional sex was a popular image in Victorian culture. (12) Interestingly, Watson uses the image of the treasure to refer to Mary, as though she is a valuable inanimate object, 'whoever had lost a treasure, I knew that night I had gained one'. This shows that like many men of his time, Watson tends to objectify women.

1. Clear point made in first paragraph, linking extract to the focus of the question. AO1

2. Idea exemplified by language analysis; terminology correctly used. AO2

3. Shows detailed knowledge and understanding of whole novel; relevant example and analysis of effects. AO1/AO2

4. Clear response to task, relevant example and good use of terminology. AO2

5. Embedded quotation analysed, good development of interpretation of language effects. AO1/AO2

6. Shows knowledge of whole novel and apt quotation analysed. AO1/AO2

7. Interpretation draws in the social context. AO2/AO3

8. Detailed language analysis to evidence a point, accurate use of terminology. AO2

9. Lacks close analysis and a quotation. AO2

10. Detailed focus on effects of specific techniques; use of relevant subject terminology. AO2

11. Focus on Conan Doyle as a writer in order to consider the text as a conscious construct. AO2

12. Response to ideas, developing an interpretation of language effects, consideration of ideas linked to context. AO1/AO2/AO3

Questions

EXAM PRACTICE

Spend 45 minutes writing a response to Question 2 on page 60.
Starting with this extract, explore how Conan Doyle presents Holmes as a complex and unusual individual. Write about:

• how Conan Doyle presents Holmes as a complex and unusual individual in this extract

• how Conan Doyle presents Holmes as a complex and unusual individual in the novel as a whole. [30 marks]

Remember to use the plan you have already prepared.

Planning a Theme Question Response

You must be able to: understand what an exam question is asking you and prepare your response.

How might an exam question be phrased?

Questions 5–8 are typical thematic questions. Some questions might ask you about character and themes – but remember that any question on theme might involve some discussion of individual characters.

Look again at Question 5 on page 61.

Starting with this extract, explore how Conan Doyle presents crime detection. Write about:

* how Conan Doyle presents crime detection in this extract
* how Conan Doyle presents crime detection in the novel as a whole.

[30 marks]

How do I work out what to do?

The focus of this question is clear: the theme of crime detection.

Use the two bullet points to structure your essay. The bullet points remind you that you should divide your answer between the extract and the rest of the novel.

For AO1, you need to show a clear understanding of the contrasting methods of Jones and Holmes. You should link these to your understanding of their differing characters based on what each does and how each speaks.

For AO2, you need to analyse the different ways Conan Doyle's use of language, form and structure help to show the contrast.

You also need to link your answer to the context of the novel to achieve your AO3 marks.

How can I plan my essay?

You have approximately 45 minutes to write your essay. This isn't long but you should spend the first five minutes writing a quick plan. This will help you to focus your thoughts and write a well-structured essay.

Try to come up with five or six ideas. Each of these ideas can then be written up as a paragraph in the essay.

You can plan in whatever way you find most useful. Some students like to just make a quick list of points and then renumber them into a logical order. Spider diagrams are particularly popular; look at the example on the opposite page.

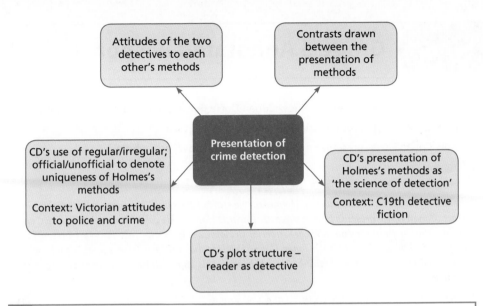

Summary

- Make sure you read the extract and the question carefully so that you know what the focus is.
- Remember to analyse how ideas are conveyed by Conan Doyle.
- Try to relate your ideas to the novel's social and historical context.

Questions

QUICK TEST
1. What key skills do you need to show in your answer?
2. What are the benefits of writing a quick plan for your essay?
3. Why is it better to have learned quotations for the exam?

EXAM PRACTICE
Plan a response to Question 6 on page 61.
Starting with this extract, explore how Conan Doyle creates a sense of tension and excitement. Write about:
- how Conan Doyle creates a sense of tension and excitement in this extract
- how Conan Doyle creates a sense of tension and excitement in the novel as a whole. [30 marks]

Starting with this extract, explore how Conan Doyle presents crime detection. Write about:
- how Conan Doyle presents crime detection in this extract
- how Conan Doyle presents crime detection in the novel as a whole.

[30 marks]

Athelney Jones doesn't think much of Holmes at the start of the novel, as we can tell from this extract. Conan Doyle presents him as sarcastic towards Holmes. He calls Holmes 'Mr Theorist' and it is clear that he thinks his methods are superior to Holmes's. His comment, 'Facts are better than mere theories' shows this. (1) With Jones, Conan Doyle is showing how Jones's methods rely on facts to confirm what he already thinks has happened – this approach leads him to wrongly arrest Thaddeus.

Holmes uses facts to deduce the truth, saying 'I never guess. ... it is destructive to the logical faculty'. Conan Doyle contrasts the two detectives and their methods in order to show Holmes is a far better detective than Jones. (2) We can see this when Holmes says, 'I will make you a present ...'. This metaphor shows that Holmes is defining the relationship between them – Holmes is generous and superior to Jones, able to give him gifts, because he knows so much more than Jones. Holmes sees connections and observes data that Jones does not see. (3)

Conan Doyle compares different methods of crime detection through Holmes and Jones. Holmes is an 'unofficial' detective (he works outside the police force) and he employs street urchins to help him find out information that the regular police force cannot. Conan Doyle uses the adjectives (4) 'official/unofficial' and 'regular/irregular' to highlight this. Holmes calls his team 'the unofficial force – the Baker Street irregulars'.

Holmes is an unusual detective because he uses a wide variety of methods. Some of these methods are also used by the regular police, such as door-to-door search and research, but others are more unusual, such as using a sniffer dog, handwriting analysis, and criminal profiling. He also uses methods which were not widely used by late Victorian detectives, such as putting himself into the criminal's shoes and using logic and probability to work out what the criminal has done and will do. (5) In this Holmes was much more modern in his approach to criminal investigation. Conan Doyle drew together different aspects of fictional detectives to create Holmes, as detective fiction was popular at this time due to an increase in violent crime. (6)

In the way he uses Watson as narrator, Conan Doyle enables readers to also become detectives. Watson is a credible narrator (7) and we trust him to tell us facts truthfully as he closely follows Holmes who pieces together the case and works out the solution. Watson is very close to Holmes, so readers also get to observe Holmes at work and observe his methods.

Athelney Jones changes his attitude to Holmes later when he says 'You are the master' (8), 'master' shows that he accepts Holmes is in charge. He also calls Holmes 'a connoisseur of crime', 'connoisseur' shows he's acknowledging that Holmes is an expert with rare skills. (9)

1. Good use of reference used but lacking use of subject terminology. AO1/AO2

2. Attempt to analyse writer's use of structure to create meaning but could be developed further. AO2

3. Accurate use of terminology to make a point about author's meaning and reference interpreted. AO2

4. Use of reference to support ideas showing knowledge of different points in the novel and good use of relevant subject terminology. AO1/AO2

5. Some understanding of how the social context relates to the writer's ideas but lacks relevant reference. AO3

6. Reference to literary context but not fully developed. AO3

7. Interpretation lacks a linked direct reference and analysis that evidences it. AO2

8. Some reference to literary content to explore how author creates meaning but lacks apt and accurate textual reference. AO2/AO3

9. Accurate reference that supports interpretation but analysis lacks specificity and use of terminology. AO1/AO2

Questions

EXAM PRACTICE

Choose a paragraph from this essay. Read it through a few times and then try to rewrite it and improve it. You might:

- replace a reference with a quotation or use a better quotation
- ensure quotations are embedded within the sentence
- provide more detailed, or a wider range of, analysis
- use more subject terminology
- link some context to the analysis more effectively.

Starting with this extract, explore how Conan Doyle presents crime detection. Write about:
- how Conan Doyle presents crime detection in this extract
- how Conan Doyle presents crime detection in the novel as a whole.

[30 marks]

Conan Doyle presents Athelney Jones as a foil for Holmes, as is evident here: Jones is noisy and combative whilst Holmes is calm and quiet. Jones is dismissive and scornful of Holmes, sneeringly calling him 'Mr Theorist', a reference to Holmes's scientific methods of crime detection, which Jones thinks are fanciful and not fact-based. (1) The epithet 'Theorist' also indicates that Jones thinks Holmes is too cerebral in his approach to detection, whereas for Jones, 'Facts are better than mere theories'. (2) Conan Doyle is inviting readers to compare the two detectives, and we are complicit in the humour of his presentation of Jones as stupid, because we know Holmes is brilliant.

Conan Doyle characterises Jones's bossy manner with heavy use of exclamations, 'You see!' and commands, 'Don't promise too much'. These convey that Jones is pompous and self-important. 'You see!' is used ironically by the writer, (3) because Jones does not see important details, whereas Holmes has 'an extraordinary genius for minutiae'. (4) The way Jones speaks to Holmes – the verb 'snaps' shows his tone is aggressive and irritable – reveals how he feels towards Holmes. He is trying hard to exert his control over Holmes. We sense that Jones feels threatened by the 'Theorist' – hence his confrontational manner. (5) This presentation of conventional crime detection as relatively unsophisticated and almost comedic aligns with a popular trope of detective fiction of the time. It was also a view that would have been familiar to Conan Doyle's Victorian readers. (6)

Conan Doyle structures the plot using several long back-story narratives that reveal facts and clues for the reader to work with. This structure itself mimics the process of crime-solving as each unfolding flashback reveals more links and connections. (7) By the time we hear Small's story, we know who stole the treasure and murdered Bartholomew, but we still do not understand why. Small's story is a 'fitting wind-up to an extremely interesting case' and here the adjective 'fitting' means not only is it appropriate or apt, but it also shows how the pieces of the puzzle 'fit' together. (8)

Holmes's methods are presented as more than just piecing together facts. He uses probability, logic, and reasoned hypothesis to arrive at the truth. He uses an array of different methods and techniques: a sniffer dog, handwriting analysis, disguise, close observation, and he employs street urchins as 'irregulars' (an epithet that characterises how they operate outside the regular police force). (9) Holmes's methods are often unconventional, as can be seen by the way he describes his role, 'unofficial consulting detective' – the adjective 'unofficial' indicating that he does not obey the rules and that he acknowledges no external authority. (10)

Conan Doyle presents Holmes's approach to criminal detection as 'the science of deduction' in the manner of a serious academic treatise. He often uses scientific language in relation to Holmes's methods to reinforce this idea, drawing on his own scientific knowledge and experience as a doctor. (11) The words 'case' and 'diagnosis' to denote the crime are taken from medicine. Holmes draws attention to this use of scientific language in relation to criminal detection when he says, 'It confirms my diagnosis, as you doctors express it'. Conan Doyle is clearly positing the view that detection is, like science, an intellectual, rigorous and systematic discipline. (12)

1. The first paragraph has a clear idea and is supported by a quotation from the extract. AO1

2. A relevant quotation is embedded as evidence. AO1

3. Detailed analysis of use of language linked to how writer creates meaning. AO2

4. Embedded quotation analysed, showing knowledge of the novel as whole. AO1/AO2

5. Interpretation explored and developed with apt use of reference as evidence. AO1

6. Reference to social context. AO3

7. Explanation of effects of structural features. AO2

8. Focus on writer's use of language to create meaning. AO2

9. Understanding of effects of language use. AO2

10. Analysis of how structure is used by the writer to create meaning linked to the theme. AO2

11. Reference to biographical context to evaluate the writer's presentation of theme and relevant use of direct references. AO2/AO3

12. Focus on writer shows consideration of the text as a conscious construct. AO2

Questions

EXAM PRACTICE
Spend 45 minutes writing an answer to Question 6 on page 61.
Starting with this extract, explore how Conan Doyle creates a sense of tension and excitement. Write about:
- how Conan Doyle creates a sense of tension and excitement in this extract
- how Conan Doyle creates a sense of tension and excitement in the novel as a whole. [30 marks]
Remember to use the plan you have already prepared.

Glossary

Abstract noun – the name of an idea, quality or concept.

Abstruse – difficult to understand.

Adjective – a word that describes a noun.

Adverb – a word that describes a verb.

Aesthete – someone who is particularly appreciative of beauty.

Alliteration – repetition of the same sound or letter at the beginning of each or most of the words in a phrase.

Anti-establishment – against the accepted political, social and economic conventions of the Establishment.

Bohemian – socially unconventional.

Caricature – an exaggerated description for comical effect.

Chaplet – a garland or circlet worn on the head.

Cliché – an overused and unoriginal phrase.

Cliffhanger – a dramatic and exciting end to a chapter, intended to increase suspense.

Climax – a decisive and intense moment in the action.

Command – a word or sentence that asks or tells people to do something.

Complicit – involved with an activity that is illegal or morally questionable.

Connotation – the idea or feeling suggested by a word (in addition to the literal meaning).

Connote – to imply or suggest an idea or feeling (in addition to the literal meaning).

Contemporary novel – a novel set at the same time as it is written.

Deduce – to reach a conclusion through reasoning and logic.

Definite article – (the) a word used before a noun when the noun is specific or particular.

Derives – is based on or originates from another word.

Ennui – boredom and general lack of interest.

Epithet – a word that characterises someone or something according to an attribute or quality.

Establishment – the dominant group of a society that holds power and authority.

Exclamation – a word or sentence that expresses strong emotion.

First-person narrator – a narrator that tells the story from his or her point of view.

Flashback – a scene or story that takes the narrative back in time from the present to the past.

Foil – a character who contrasts with another character in order to highlight the second character's qualities.

Foreshadow – an early hint or clue of what is to come later in a story.

Formal register – a tone and style of writing that is appropriate for official or public occasions and audiences.

Gothic – in fiction, a style of writing intended to produce emotions of horror, terror and other extremes.

Idealised – a presentation that is better than reality, or perfect.

Image – a mental picture formed by words.

Imagery – words used to create a picture in the imagination.

Imperialist – relating to the rule or authority of an empire.

Implicit – something that is suggested rather than directly expressed.

Irony – something that seems the opposite of what was expected.

Juxtapose – two or more elements placed close together, or side by side, for contrast.

Literal – the most basic meaning of a word without metaphor, exaggeration or other allusion.

Literary device – a technique used by a writer to create a particular effect.

Metaphor – a descriptive technique, using comparison to say one thing is another.

Metonymy – using the name of one object to refer to another to which it is closely related.

Narrator – the person who tells the story.

Objectivity – lack of bias, judgement or prejudice.

Omniscient – able to know and see everything.

Other – a person, thing, or place that is different from what is known.

Parallelism – the use of elements in a sentence that correspond to the same grammatical construction.

Pathetic fallacy – the attribution of human feelings to inanimate objects or animals, especially in nature.

Personification – the attribution of human characteristics to something that is not human.

Phrase – a group of words expressing a particular idea.

Physiognomy – the assessment of a person's character or personality from the appearance of the person's body, especially the face.

Plausibility – having the appearance of truth or reason.

Plethoric – (medical term) ruddy, swollen with blood.

Polymath – someone who has knowledge of a wide range of subjects.

Pot-boiler – a low-quality artistic work produced quickly to make money.

Prescribe – to state a rule with authority.

Pseudo-science – beliefs or practices that are mistakenly thought to have scientific basis.

Recount – (noun) a narrative that tells of past events in the order they happened.

Rhetorical question – a question asked for effect rather than in expectation of an answer.

Sarcastic/sarcasm – using irony in order to mock or criticise.

Simile – a descriptive technique that compares one thing to another thing using 'like' or 'as'.

Social inequality – the uneven distribution of resources in a society.

Status quo – the existing state of affairs.

Stereotype – a set or simplified idea about what someone or something is like.

Subjective point of view – an opinion based on opinion rather than fact.

Symbol/symbolise – an object, colour, person or thing that represents a specific idea or meaning.

Symbolic – involving the use of symbols.

Synonym – a word of phrase that means exactly or nearly the same as another word or phrase.

Term – a word or phrase used to denote an idea or concept in a particular branch of study.

Touchstone – a standard or criterion by which things are recognised or judged.

Truism – an undisputed or self-evident truth.

Verb – a doing, feeling, thinking or being word.

Verisimilitude – the appearance of being true or real.

Answers

5. The Andaman Islands.

Exam Practice

Answers might focus on the conversation between Holmes and Watson as they follow Toby through London, how Holmes tells Watson how he has fitted the clues and facts together as a basis for his reasoned hypothesis about what happened prior to Bartholomew's murder. Analysis might include how Conan Doyle uses the language of science for Holmes's deductions ('hypothesis', 'facts', 'reasoning') and how Holmes insists that his methods are logical and rational, not theatrical or mysterious. He uses 'obvious' to emphasise this idea.

Pages 4–5
Quick Test

1. He asks Holmes to examine and deduce facts about his watch.
2. 10 years before the present day of the novel.
3. A large pearl.
4. Captain Morstan's friend.
5. The writer of the anonymous letter.

Exam Practice

Answers might focus on Watson's admiration for Holmes's mind, Holmes's **ennui**, the contrast between Watson's emotional nature and Holmes's lack of empathy. Analysis could include: the effect of Watson's use of the phrase 'great powers' in relation to Holmes's mental powers; how he is 'irritated' by Holmes's criticism of his writing style and his diffidence to challenge Holmes, all of which show Watson's sensitivity.

Pages 6–7
Quick Test

1. Jonathan Small, Mahomet Singh, Abdullah Khan, Dost Akbar.
2. Prize-fighters.
3. A man's face.
4. Thaddeus Sholto.
5. In a secret garret.

Exam Practice

Answers might focus on Watson's sense of disorientation and growing anxiety as they drive to south London, the oddity of Thaddeus' rooms, the strange behaviour of Sholto and what we learn about Bartholomew's character. Analysis could include: Watson's use of 'monster tentacles' to describe the threatening spread of the city as they drive through it; the unsettling contrast between the opulence of Thaddeus' apartment and the grimness of the house it is in; Thaddeus' striking description of the face at the window 'bearded, hairy' with 'wild cruel eyes' that is intended to convey terror.

Pages 8–9
Quick Test

1. It is locked from the inside.
2. Through the keyhole.
3. They are child-sized.
4. By a rope from the window.
5. A sniffer dog called Toby.

Exam Practice

Answers might focus on Holmes's use of a magnifying glass and observation of minute details as he ascends the stairs to the room, and his piecing together of facts, observations and deductions. Analysis might include Watson's detailed description of Holmes at work examining 'shapeless smudges' and how repetition of the word 'slow' emphasises the careful, methodical way he works. 'Links' and 'connected' reinforce the sense that Holmes works scientifically and logically.

Pages 10–11
Quick Test

1. They have splayed toes.
2. A handkerchief soaked in creosote.
3. *Aurora*.

Pages 12–13
Quick Test

1. The Irregulars cannot find her.
2. At Jacobson's Yard.
3. Sailor.
4. Holmes will interview Small; Watson will take the treasure box to Mary.
5. His wooden leg gets stuck in the mud after the *Aurora* hits the river bank.

Exam Practice

Answers might focus on: the sense of suspense as they wait for the *Aurora*; the sense of speed as the furnaces go at full pelt; the Thames locations mentioned; the shouts and cries; and Watson's description of his own excitement. Analysis might include: the use of personification for the action of the furnaces 'roared', 'like a great metallic heart'; the urgency of Holmes's 'pile it on!', and the uncharacteristic show of his emotion indicated by exclamations; Watson's use of the phrase 'wild thrill' and how the adjectives 'mad' and 'flying' convey his excitement.

Pages 14–15
Quick Test

1. To find safety after his employers were killed by Indian rebels.
2. Abdullah Khan.
3. Hid it in a wall in the fort at Agra.
4. Sholto had lost heavily at cards and needed money.
5. Small saved Tonga's life.

Exam Practice

Answers might focus on: how Small's story links with the beginning when Mary showed Holmes the map signed by 'the four'; how Small's story confirms Holmes's hypothesis and proves he was right, which is satisfying for the reader; Small's sense of loyalty comes across strongly in his story and this aligns to a key theme of the novel. Analysis might include: how Small says 'I have no wish to hold it [his story] back' and Holmes invites his confession so that they might judge how far 'justice' was on his side; Small's sense of fairness and loyalty indicated by the phrases 'black or blue … we all go together' (showing race colour-blindness) and his looking after Tonga, despite his fierceness.

Pages 16–17
Quick Test

1. Dr Watson.
2. First-person narrator.
3. Four days in September 1888.
4. Mary Morstan, Thaddeus Sholto and Jonathan Small.
5. To reveal important information from the past that helps to solve the case.

Exam Practice

Answers might focus on the strategic placement of the three flashbacks in the structure: Mary's sets up the mystery; Thaddeus prepares us for the discovery of the murdered Bartholomew; Small's gives a sense of completion and proves that Holmes was completely correct, which is satisfying for the reader. Analysis could include how Mary and Thaddeus both refer to 'facts' and Small to 'truth', showing that all three express a wish to be truthful. Small's flashback is also like a confession or even a defence as if he were on trial in a court of law.

Pages 18–19

Quick Test

1. He finds it depressing.
2. As 'monster tentacles' of 'dull brick' terraces.
3. The Hindoo servant; Tonga.
4. Two from: Mr Sherman, Mordecai and Mrs Smith, McMurdo, Wiggins.
5. They seem to like and trust him.

Exam Practice

Answers might focus on: the suitability of contemporary London as a setting for a crime/mystery story as the city was crime-ridden, with millions of people living in close contact, many of them in poor conditions; how naming real locations adds authenticity; we have the sense that the characters are really living in London. Analysis might mention: Conan Doyle's use of **personification** ('monster tentacles'), which has the effect of making the city almost another character; Watson's use of pathetic fallacy ('mud-coloured clouds drooped sadly') and other poetic devices used to describe the Strand.

Pages 20–21

Quick Test

1. The 'Jack the Ripper' murders.
2. Rapid population growth, poverty, London's growing trade and affluence, widespread drunkenness and drug-use.
3. 1829.
4. The first policemen, so called because the force was set up by Robert Peel.
5. The assessment of character or personality from a person's appearance, especially the face.

Exam Practice

Answers might focus on: the presentation of Jones, the representative of law enforcement, as pompous, clumsy and slow compared to Holmes; how Holmes characterises himself as a detective working outside the official force but when he needs brute force and officialdom to enforce the law, he calls in the police. Analysis might include: Conan Doyle's use of adjectives official/unofficial and regular/irregular/auxiliary to indicate the difference between Holmes and Jones but the two work together successfully to enforce the law. When Holmes uses the epithet 'energetic' to describe Jones he is being sarcastic, because Jones's great energy is often misplaced, and it also implies that although Jones is energetic, he is not intelligent.

Pages 22–23

Quick Test

1. They were fascinated by them but also feared and distrusted them.
2. India came under British rule.
3. Captain Morstan, Major Sholto.
4. On a plantation near Agra.
5. He exhibited him at fairs.

Exam Practice

Answers might focus on: the Empire as a backdrop for flashback events (the Indian Rebellion, the stolen Agra treasure); the presentation of and treatment of Tonga; attitudes towards wealth and opulence associated with imperial expansion. Analysis might include: how Small's description of the Indian rebels as 'black devils' shows he thinks they are evil yet he is willing to exploit Tonga as a 'black cannibal' to earn a living; how Small's attitude encapsulates the Victorian fear/fascination with other cultures and races.

Pages 24–25

Quick Test

1. Crime was on the rise and Victorians were fascinated by criminals, criminal cases, and detection.
2. To thrill readers.
3. The fictional detective.
4. They had logical, credible plots in which everything is explained; they used forensic techniques of detection; they involved readers in the detective process.
5. Gothic fiction.

Exam Practice

Answers might focus on: Conan Doyle's creation of Holmes, a brilliant, enigmatic detective with unusual methods who operates outside official law enforcement; he includes lurid and sometimes gory details; fast-moving and exciting plots; good conquers evil and justice is done at the end. Analysis might include: reference to Holmes's insistence that all will be 'clear enough', and the necessary qualities for a detective (powers of observation and deduction) – there is nothing that cannot be easily explained through logic and reason; how he uses his 'genius for minutiae' (ability to observe details and then connect them) to solve the crime; how Conan Doyle places clues such as a 'hole in the roof!' to encourage the reader actively to speculate and piece together what happened.

Pages 26–27

Quick Test

1. Upper, middle and lower (working) classes.
2. It was becoming easier to travel, books and newspapers were more affordable, and more people were educated.
3. Order, morality, retaining established class difference, the authority of law.
4. Thaddeus Sholto.
5. Any one from: McMurdo, Mr Sherman, the Smiths.

Exam Practice

Answers might focus on: Watson's attitude to Mary – when he thinks she is an heiress, she is out of reach to him socially and economically, but this changes once the treasure is lost. Analysis might include: reference to 'might she not look upon me as a mere vulgar treasure-seeker?', showing Watson's acute sense of the inequalities of class ('vulgar', meaning crass or sordid, tells us that he has social anxieties about how others might view him); use of the treasure as a symbol of different things to different characters – to Watson it is a 'golden barrier' (a symbol of class divide) whereas to Small it represents social mobility. Analysis might also include the gulf between Thaddeus and the working-class policeman indicated by the distaste in Thaddeus' statement.

Pages 28–29

Quick Test

1. In *Lippincott's Magazine*.
2. Cliffhanger.
3. To create a sense of verisimilitude.
4. Dr Watson.

Exam Practice

Answers might focus on: choosing to make the narrator a doctor (same profession as himself); his need to present Holmes's methods as rational, logical and scientific (reflecting Conan Doyle's own interests); his research skills put to use in writing accurately about London. Analysis might include: many instances of the words drawn from scientific and empirical enquiry – 'data', 'methods', 'results', 'hypothesis', 'facts' – to describe Holmes's methods, reflecting the author's scientific and medical background; reference to how Holmes had earlier disliked Watson's romanticised account of the previous case (*A Study in Scarlet*).

Pages 30–31

Quick Test

1. He takes cocaine.
2. It gives him objectivity.
3. He plays the violin.
4. His 'masterly manner'.
5. He instructs Watson to fetch Toby.

Answers

Exam Practice
Answers might focus on Holmes's approach to detective work as a challenging puzzle ('cryptogram') that can be worked out. Emotions have no role in this approach as it is an 'exact science' but this can lead him to blunder as when he upsets Watson after examining his watch. Analysis might include focusing on the adjectives Holmes uses: 'abstruse' (difficult to understand) 'abstract' (theoretical or academic) and 'exact' (detailed, precise) – all words that emphasise how Holmes values the intellectual and rational over emotion.

Pages 32–33
Quick Test
1. So that Watson conveys important facts about the case to the reader.
2. 'Mr Theorist'.
3. Technical monographs.
4. He can be both lazy ('fine loafer') and energetic ('pretty spry sort of fellow').
5. To show that Holmes has not changed as a character.

Exam Practice
Answers might focus on: the duality and complexity of Holmes's character, indicated by periods of indolence and hyperactivity, and by the contradiction between his insistence on the importance of cold rationality and his poetic description of the cloud. These demonstrate that Holmes is not a one-dimensional character. Answers might also mention: Holmes's insight into the criminal mind but lack of human empathy; his ease with all classes but abrupt lack of social graces; he can be highly entertaining when he wants to be but morose and sullen at other times; his artistic side (the violin). Analysis might include: Conan Doyle's use of Watson's as narrator/friend/chronicler to identify Holmes's contradictions and complexities; the parallelism in 'never ... tired by work ... idleness exhausts me completely' **juxtaposes** twin concepts of work/idleness with never tired/exhausted and wittily upends the conventional view of the two concepts, showing Holmes's unconventional nature. Duality is also apparent in the 'cold reason' versus 'emotional' quotation – Holmes's poetic and imaginative side is shown in his simile comparing a pink cloud to a flamingo's feather.

Pages 34–35
Quick Test
1. He can show Holmes at work from close perspective.
2. Mary Morstan.
3. Because she is an heiress to a great fortune.
4. He thinks Watson romanticised it.
5. His arrogant superiority.

Exam Practice
Answers might focus on how Watson's ordinariness makes Holmes look even more brilliant and his emotions and humanity accentuate Holmes's coldness and lack of emotion. These qualities make Watson the better choice as narrator – he is able to engage readers, use techniques to keep readers excited and involved; Watson's respect and admiration for Holmes colours our impressions of the detective's unusual brilliance. Analysis might include looking closely at how Conan Doyle uses language in the exchanges between the two; Holmes uses commands, 'Look here!', and chides Watson as if he were a wayward pupil, 'You will not apply my precept' (principle).

Pages 36–37
Quick Test
1. He is very certain of what is right/good and what is evil/wrong; he is acutely aware of the class divide and the importance of wealth.
2. He feels guilty for being happy that Mary will not inherit great wealth.
3. One from: his reaction when Small describes the murder of Achmet; his reaction to Tonga's appearance.
4. It might damage his (brilliant) mind.
5. It emphasises Holmes's brilliance, enables the reader to see Holmes's faults, and it humanises Watson. Because he is critical of Holmes, the reader trusts Watson's account.

Exam Practice
Answers might focus on: Watson sometimes tests and questions Holmes and marvels at his friend's genius; Watson is Holmes's assistant and helper but isn't blind to his faults; Holmes likes to have an audience (Watson) but his arrogance sometimes irritates his friend. Analysis might include: Watson observes that Holmes is an 'automaton' ('mechanical', 'unfeeling') and this is reinforced by the adjective 'inhuman', showing that Watson is well aware of his friend's lack of humanity. Watson's inner doubt about whether Holmes is right is shown by the rhetorical question: 'radical' has two meanings – 'fundamental' and 'extreme' so by using this adjective Watson indicates that Holmes's unconventionality makes him feel uneasy.

Pages 38–39
Quick Test
1. She is more concerned that Thaddeus is released than about the treasure.
2. Because he is in love with her.
3. She brings the map from her father's desk to show Holmes.
4. Because it enables Watson to declare his love and propose to her.

Exam Practice
Answers might focus on the fact that Watson, the narrator, is in love with Mary; it indicates Watson's emotional and romantic nature; it fits the Victorian stereotype of virtuous women in popular romantic fiction of the time; it is a contrast to the greedy, evil male characters (e.g. Sholto, Small), so has a moral dimension. Analysis might include: the adjectives Watson uses to describe Mary – 'calm', 'angelic', 'weak'; her physical weakness as shown by her trembling lip and quivering hand; her passivity (fainting); and how she is introduced as a 'wronged woman' – acted upon by greedy men, rather than acting herself.

Pages 40–41
Quick Test
1. Major Sholto.
2. It is luxuriously furnished with Oriental objects.
3. They frighten him.
4. He felt guilty that she had not received the inheritance she was due.

Exam Practice
Answers might focus on the oddity of Thaddeus' character – he is a wealthy eccentric, representative of the spoils of Empire, unlike any other character in the novel, and his strong sense of justice/morality leads him to contact Mary. His fear of the lower orders is indicative of social change in late Victorian England. Analysis might include: reference to Thaddeus' odd appearance, writhing hands, and jerking features; his pride in his own taste and sensitivity; the image created of him as weak and vulnerable in the description 'helpless appealing expression of a terrified child.'

Pages 42–43
Quick Test
1. He is red-faced, burly and stout.
2. With sneering sarcasm.
3. Because he realises he has arrested the wrong people and that Holmes is correct.

4. He organises the police launch and policemen.
5. No – his self-importance re-emerges.

Exam Practice

Answers might focus on: how Jones is a foil for Holmes from the start; he is used to gently poke fun at standards of crime detection at this time; he is an amiable buffoon and unlikely to change or learn anything from Holmes. Analysis might include: reference to adjectives describing Jones physically – 'burly', 'plethoric' – contrasted to those used elsewhere for Holmes ('gaunt', 'hawk-like features', 'glittering eyes'). Even though he calls Holmes 'master of the situation' (which echoes Watson earlier), Watson notes his earlier sneering manner and that old 'airs' return after the capture.

Pages 44–45

Quick Test

1. To confirm that Holmes's hypotheses were correct.
2. Because of the hardships he had suffered, especially the betrayal and imprisonment after stealing the treasure.
3. He thought he deserved the treasure because he had helped steal it, even though it involved murdering someone.
4. It exactly matches the description of Andaman natives Holmes read in the gazetteer, which characterises them as violent, vicious, immoral, untrustworthy and cannibals.

Exam Practice

Answers might focus on how Small earned Tonga's loyalty by saving his life, used Tonga's resources to escape, then exploited him by exhibiting him as a black cannibal, and later beat him when Tonga murdered Bartholomew (which was what Tonga thought Small wanted). Analysis might include how Small's treatment of Tonga is aligned with an imperialist attitude that sees colonisation as a source of obtaining more power and wealth through exploitation. Analysis could also include: Small's simile comparing Tonga to a snake, suggesting he cannot be trusted and is inherently dangerous; Small's use of 'little' and 'poor' to describe for Tonga – these adjectives acknowledge Tonga's vulnerability but also may indicate a patronising attitude towards a man Small considers of less value than himself.

Pages 46–47

Quick Test

1. He knows Watson has sent a telegram; he tells Watson about his brother by observing his watch.
2. That a wooden-legged man made the print.
3. They refer to crime detection as a science.
4. When he tracks down Small.

Exam Practice

Answers might focus on the range of methods Holmes uses, some of which are standard detective methods (handwriting analysis and door-to-door searches) whereas others are more unusual (using street urchins as spies, applying probability and criminal profiling). Analysis might include: reference to the scientific and statistical aspects of Holmes's enquiry and methods – he is meticulous about detail ('minutiae') and uses this to form hypotheses, which are not 'guesses' but logical deductions; he uses probability to decide a course of action when he is not completely sure (which is not the same as guessing). It is the combination of these things, along with his ability to find connections, that forms his unique genius for detective work.

Pages 48–49

Quick Test

1. He has dark skin, venomous eyes, black hair.
2. It is traditionally when strange, violent or evil events occur.
3. She did not receive her father's share of the treasure.
4. It is faulty. He thinks his hardship makes him deserving of the treasure. He thinks violence is justified by violence.

Exam Practice

Answers might focus on: how Tonga is presented as an evil force because he is from the Andaman Islands, he looks evil and he possesses deadly weapons; how Small's appearance somewhat resembles Tonga's; how Small is set up as the villain from the start – later we learn he is a murderer and wished to

kill Sholto; how Conan Doyle uses Gothic imagery to create an atmosphere of evil. Analysis might look at how Conan Doyle focuses on the eyes as descriptors of emotional expression: Watson's description of Tonga's 'venomous, menacing eyes' compared with Thaddeus' description of Small's 'wild cruel eyes', and Watson's later description of Small's eyes that 'blazed' when he saw the 'fury and passion of the man'. The idea that evil can be seen in a person's expression fits with Victorian belief that a person's appearance showed their character.

Pages 50–51

Quick Test

1. Fascination because they were strange and different, and fear because they could not be trusted and were different.
2. Power by rule over other nations, and wealth by plundering their resources.
3. It is a symbol of Eastern wealth to be plundered at will.
4. That any insurrection or challenge to British law must be put down; that the native people were violent and untrustworthy and must be controlled.

Exam Practice

Answers might focus on the belief that the natives of a state under imperial rule could not be trusted because they were too different from the British, as demonstrated by the description in the gazetteer and by Small. Analysis might include: close reference to the official description of the Andaman natives as 'intractable and fierce', and Small's understanding of Tonga as a 'blood-thirsty imp', that is, an uncivilised savage, even though he recognises Tonga's loyalty and indeed exploits it – he is the first to escape prison and then to make a living. Small controls Tonga through force, just as the British controlled the rebels in India.

Pages 52–53

Quick Test

1. It says that greed is a sin that corrupts men.
2. Major Sholto.
3. Small.
4. By comparing the attitudes of Mary, who is unmoved by wealth (absence of greed) with Small and Sholto, who are controlled by it (greed).
5. Mary Morstan, Thaddeus Sholto.

Exam Practice

Answers might focus on: Sholto's admission that greed has been his besetting sin and his feeling of guilt that his own greed prevented Mary from receiving her deserved share; how greed came between the Sholto twins and was the basis of an argument that led to Captain Morstan's death; how Small's greed caused him to join 'the four' and that he approached Sholto to find the treasure because he knew Sholto was motivated by greed. Analysis might include: how Conan Doyle identifies greed as a mortal sin (avarice being one of the seven deadly sins), using the theme of greed to give the novel a moral compass; how he links evil and greed; how he contrasts evil/greed with the angelic, virtuous Mary who is not motivated by greed at all.

Pages 54–55

Quick Test

1. One from: Thaddeus, Achmet, Major Sholto.
2. Gothic.
3. It means he feels no fear.
4. He alternates faster-paced passages with slower, reflective ones.

Exam Practice

Answers might reference different types of fear: Watson's class-based fear of not being good enough for Mary; physical fear (Sholto's fear that Small will kill him); fear of wrongful accusation (Sholto hiding Morstan's body, Thaddeus' reaction when he is arrested); fear of the uncivilised and violence (Thaddeus' fear of uneducated, lower-class people, Watson's

Answers

fear of Tonga). Analysis might explore how Conan Doyle explores fear through different dimensions: as a consequence of sin (greed); as a result of social segmentation and challenge at this time; as an aspect of imperialism; and how he presents fear as weakness whilst its absence is strength. Analysis might also explore how Conan Doyle portrays Achmet's physical fear in the simile 'like a mouse', and uses Gothic imagery to instil fear in readers, for example, the adjectives 'horrible' and 'unnatural' to describe the expression on the face of Bartholomew's corpse.

Pages 56–57
Quick Test
1. 'The four'.
2. Major Sholto.
3. His loyalty to the three Sikh troopers.
4. Tonga.
5. That criminals can also be complex people.

Exam Practice
Answers might focus on the importance of loyalty to Sholto: he has a keen sense of loyalty with regard to the oath he took to the four; he acknowledges Tonga's loyalty; he becomes obsessed with revenge on Sholto for what he sees as betrayal. For Small, loyalty is law and betrayal a sin. Analysis might consider why Conan Doyle has Small use the adjective 'staunch', meaning loyal and trusty, to describe Tonga when Holmes had earlier described the need for two 'staunch' policemen on the police launch.

Pages 62–63
Quick Test
1. Understanding of the whole text, specific analysis and terminology, awareness of the relevance of context, a well-structured essay and accurate writing.
2. Planning focuses your thoughts and allows you to produce a well-structured essay.
3. Quotations give you more opportunities to do specific AO2 analysis.

Exam Practice
Ideas might include the following: Holmes finds ordinary life unbearably dull, needing cocaine to stimulate his mind and needing criminal cases for the same reason; addicted to brainwork; approaches crime from a unique perspective as a scientific enquiry; exploration of his scientific methods – he is an 'expert' and 'specialist', that is, he is different to ordinary people ('peculiar powers' means he knows he is unique). Mention other examples of his complexity and individuality: violin player; relationship to Watson; moments of poetry; well-read (references to French and German philosophers) and ability to converse on a range of subjects; depending on mood can be either entertaining/have a sense of humour or morose; attitudes to women and lower classes; lack of social graces; ability to get inside the mind of the criminal.

Pages 66–67 and 72–73
Exam Practice
Use the mark scheme below to self-assess your strengths and weaknesses. Work up from the bottom, putting a tick by things you have fully accomplished, a ½ by skills that are in place but need securing and underlining areas that need particular development. The estimated grade boundaries are included so you can assess your progress towards your target grade.

Pages 68–69
Quick Test
1. Understanding of the whole text, specific analysis and terminology, awareness of the relevance of context, a well-structured essay and accurate writing.
2. Planning focuses your thoughts and allows you to produce a well-structured essay.
3. Quotations give you more opportunities to do specific AO2 analysis.

Exam Practice
Ideas might include the following: personification of the launch; use of exclamations from the usually unemotional Holmes; description of the chase – sense of speed (verbs 'flashed', 'thundered' and the visual image 'swirl of white foam'), sounds ('cried' 'hailed'), movement ('rolling waves') – all piled up together to give a sense of frenetic energy and exhilaration; tension at Pondicherry Lodge; tension of waiting for news from the Irregulars; excitement and tension when Tonga takes aim.

Grade	AO1 (12 marks)	AO2 (12 marks)	AO3 (6 marks)
6–7+	A convincing, well-structured essay that answers the question fully. Quotations and references are well chosen and integrated into sentences. The response covers the whole novel.	Analysis of the full range of Conan Doyle's methods. Thorough exploration of the effects of these methods. Accurate range of subject terminology.	Exploration is linked to specific aspects of the novel's contexts to show a detailed understanding.
4–5	A clear essay that always focuses on the exam question. Quotations and references support ideas effectively. The response refers to different points in the novel.	Explanation of Conan Doyle's different methods. Clear understanding of the effects of these methods. Accurate use of subject terminology.	References to relevant aspects of context show a clear understanding.
2–3	The essay has some good ideas that are mostly relevant. Some quotations and references are used to support the ideas.	Identification of some different methods used by Conan Doyle to convey meaning. Some subject terminology.	Some awareness of how ideas in the novel link to its context.